Leaving Lymon

Leaving Lymon

LESA CLINE-RANSOME

HOLIDAY HOUSE   NEW YORK

Library of Congress Cataloging-in-Publication Data

Names: Cline-Ransome, Lesa, author.
Title: Leaving Lymon / Lesa Cline-Ransome.
Description: First edition. | New York : Holiday House, [2020] | Summary:
Raised by his grandparents, first in Mississippi then in Wisconsin,
ten-year-old Lymon moves to Chicago in 1945 to live with the mother he
never knew, while yearning for his father.
Identifiers: LCCN 2019011659 | ISBN 9780823444427 (hardcover)
Subjects: | CYAC: Family problems—Fiction. | Moving,
Household—Fiction. | African Americans—Fiction. | Milwaukee (Wis.) —
History—20th century—Fiction. | Chicago (Ill.) —History—20th century—Fiction.
Classification: LCC PZ7.C622812 Le 2019 | DDC [Fic]—dc23
LC record available at https://lccn.loc.gov/2019011659

In memory of my own Auntie Vera (Ransom):
kind, independent, supportive and a rock for us all

September 30, 1929–July 3, 2019

Leaving Lymon

Daddy

ONE

Parchman Farm
Sunflower County, Mississippi 1938

MA and Grandpops didn't tell me nothing 'cept we were going on the train. From our house I could sometimes hear the train whistle on quiet nights. Grandpops used to tell me stories about trains that carry people to places far away to a town I thought was called *North*. Turns out that wasn't the name of a town at all, just a place people bought a ticket to.

Ma made a mess of food. She spent all Saturday cooking, and the house smelled like frying grease and pickles and chocolate cake. I told her twice I was hungry, just to get a taste of something, but she hit me so hard on my backside, I stopped asking after that. Way past supper and bedtime, Grandpops came in my room whispering.

"Lymon, c'mon now. Time we get going." He dressed me quiet in my church shirt and pants, wrapped my blanket 'round my shoulders, and carried me out to his truck. I remember the truck smelled like all the food Ma had been cooking, and that smell woke me up good.

"We going on the train now?" I asked.

"Sure are," said Grandpops. Ma just closed her eyes, laid her head back against the seat, and didn't say nothing. I thought she was tired from all the cooking.

We drove quiet through the night till we pulled up to a small building.

"Here we are, Jackson Depot," Grandpops said.

Grandpops lifted me out first, and kept my blanket 'round my shoulders. Then he helped down Ma. Last he got the basket of food Ma made. While Grandpops stood in line for tickets, I looked 'round at all the other folks. Most looking as tired as Ma and nearly all with food and bags and packages. The ladies had on fancy dresses. I grabbed Grandpops' hand tight when I saw the lights from the train and heard its loud whistle when it pulled into the station, huffing and puffing smoke. Back home it sounded like a whisper, but here, it sounded it like a long scream. I covered my ears, and Grandpops laughed. I nearly peed myself, I was aching so bad to get on that train.

"Stop that jumping." Ma snatched my arm.

The train was so tall, I didn't know how we were gonna get all the way up there, but then a man opened a door and let down stairs. Grandpops helped me up the steps and I walked into the train car. It looked like it went on forever, and when we walked through, I ran my hand on the backs of the seats we passed. I didn't care it was crowded and hot with people smells and food smells. Felt good to be going somewhere new. Skinny as I was, I sat on the hard seat between Grandpops and Ma.

Train man yelled, "All aboard the Midnight Special!"

"When we gonna get there?" I asked Grandpops.

"You go on and sleep now. We got a ways. Be morning before we pull in."

Heard Ma suck her teeth and look away.

I told myself I'd stay wake the whole time so I wouldn't miss a thing. Liked hearing the train men in uniforms ask for tickets, and listen to the folks talking and babies crying. But it was so warm and tight in my seat, I couldn't keep my eyes open. I woke with my head in Grandpops' lap and heard the conductor shouting, "Parchman Farm."

"This it?" I asked, sitting up straight.

Everybody got up to get off the train and there was a beat-up bus waiting and we all got on that. Wasn't near as fun as being on the train, but Grandpops said, "Not long now," and I mashed my face against the cool of the window.

———◆———

In the back of the bus, someone started singing a song I sometimes heard in church. Few others joined in. Out the window, I saw rows and rows and rows of cotton as we drove up a long road and under a gate.

As soon as we stepped off the bus, I heard someone shout, "Pops!" And there was my daddy. His face was so fuzzy in my head, I almost forgot what he looked like. He was smiling big and walking fast toward us. His black-and-white-striped pajamas looked too big for him, and I heard Ma breathe in fast.

"Ma," he said, kissing her on the cheek.

"Grady," is all she said.

But Grandpops pulled him in close and hard. "How you makin' it, son?"

"I'm making it, Pops, I'm making it…."

"And who is this young man growing tall as a weed?" Daddy asked looking down at me.

"I'm Lymon," I told him.

"I know who you are, boy!" He laughed and swung me up high.

Seemed like a big party. All the men there dressed in the striped pajamas like Daddy. There was music playing from a radio, and couples were dancing close and kissing too.

"Stop staring," Ma told me, and moved me away.

We laid down my blanket under a tree, and Ma put out all the food she made. Daddy and Grandpops talked and talked. Ma barely ate.

"You ain't hungry, Ma?" I asked her. My belly was hurtin' 'cause I ate too many deviled eggs. She didn't answer. Just looked out past the trees. Daddy showed us where he and the other men slept. In one big house with beds all lined up next to each other. He held my hand when we walked. It was hard and dry and cracked, but it still felt good holding mine. After Ma cleaned up the food and cut the cake, Daddy took out a harmonica. He took his hands and made a cup around it and made music come out that sounded a lot like the train whistle back at the depot. As he was playing, more and more folks came over, standing 'round my daddy. His face got wetter and wetter the more he played. Folks were clapping and moving to the music. But then the white men with guns came over too, and folks quieted down some. When Daddy finished playing, one of the white men stepped forward.

"Your boy got talent," he said to Grandpops.

Grandpops looked down. "Yessir," he said quiet.

"He behave hisself in here, maybe he make you proud one day, right, boy?" he said to my daddy.

"Yessir," my daddy said, and put his harmonica back in his pajama pocket.

Folks started moving away. I went and sat up close to my daddy.

"So how's my Lymon doing?" he asked smiling down at me.

"Good, Daddy."

"How's your momma?" he asked. I shrugged.

"You know he ain't seen her since she left. Why you asking foolishness? She's there and he's here. That's how she's doing." Ma started coughing like she do whenever she starts yelling.

"Alright now, Lenore. You getting yourself all worked up. Ain't a need for all that today. He's just asking a question is all."

Ma got quiet again.

"Heard she went up to Chicago with her sister not too long ago," Grandpops said into Daddy's ear. "Got another one on the way."

Daddy whistled through his teeth and shook his head.

"Vera and Shirley send their best," Grandpops told Daddy. "Clark got a good job at the new foundry in Milwaukee. They told us to come up and join 'em."

"Y'all thinking about going?" Daddy asked.

"Nah, I can't get this woman to leave Vicksburg for nothing in the world, right, Lenore?" Grandpops laughed, looking at Ma.

I saw a little smile at the corner of Ma's mouth. First one all day.

"Ain't no need dragging my tail all the way to Milwaukee when I got all I need right here in Mississippi."

"She's talking about me." Grandpops leaned over and kissed Ma a big kiss on her cheek.

She laughed then. "Stop that fuss, Frank. You are a fool."

One of the white man started clanging a bell and told everybody visiting time was over. Folks started picking up all their food and fixings and saying goodbye and kissing even more. I couldn't help but stare then. And Ma didn't stop me. Someone was crying loud.

We stood up, and I hugged my daddy tight 'round the waist. "You coming home with us?" I asked.

I saw the water in his eyes. "Not today, son, but I'll be home soon," is all he said.

Grandpops took my hand. "Come on, Lymon."

When Daddy bent down to kiss Ma I heard him say, "Don't

bring him back here no more. I don't never want to see him inside this place again."

Ma pulled away from Daddy. "You should have thought about that before—"

"Hush, Lenore!" Grandpops said, mad.

Me and Ma walked onto the bus as Daddy and Grandpops hugged goodbye. When the bus pulled down the long dusty road, my daddy was the last one in a line of men in pajamas walking back into their house.

TWO

Vicksburg, Mississippi 1939

I knew it was Friday when Grandpops started cleaning his guitar. He worked all week at the mill, coming home every night tired and dirty. Ma had supper ready, and soon as Grandpops washed up, we'd eat. After the supper dishes were put up, Ma sat out front with me and Grandpops, watching the lightning bugs, and doing her crocheting, Grandpops talking a mile a minute and plucking his favorite songs on his guitar, Ma saying every now and then, "mmm-hmmm," and tapping her foot. But on Friday nights, Grandpops didn't eat supper with us. He'd come home, same as always, but he'd wash up, then polish up his guitar, check the strings, and one by one, his men friends would come by the house with guitars and harmonicas, one banjo. Ma would stay in the kitchen making sandwiches and put them on a big ole plate and bring out some soda pop to the front room. Later it got, after the sandwiches and pop were gone, the men took out jars of other drinks they passed around. When it was still early, Grandpops would let me sit with them in the front room and listen. Sometimes they did more talking than playing. But on a good Friday, when everybody was in the mood for playing, it could go on nearly all night.

The man with the banjo was Mr. Joe from church. He came every week with the same old beat-up overalls and worn-through shirt. He looked old enough to be my grandpops' daddy, but if you closed your eyes when he sang, his voice sounded young and sweet as a girl's. He hiked one leg up on the chair while he played his banjo. Tilted his head back and sang:

> *Got to New York this mornin', just about half-past nine*
> *Got to New York this mornin', just about half-past nine*
> *Hollerin' one mornin' in Avalon, couldn't hardly keep*
> *from cryin'*
> *Avalon, my hometown, always on my mind*
> *Avalon, my hometown, always on my mind*
> *Pretty momma's in Avalon, want me there all the time...*

On those nights, I'd see Ma standing in the doorway of the kitchen, her hand tapping her thigh in time to the music.

My grandpops would strum along behind Mister Joe's singing and you could hear the other men saying low, "c'mon now, Joe," and "tell it," just like we were in church on Sunday morning. If it got too good, I couldn't stop myself from clapping. One time Grandpops pulled me onto his lap.

"You remember that song we been working on?" he asked.

I nodded.

"Go on ahead then," he said. Grandpops set his guitar on my legs, and I started right in playing. I looked around and all the men were nodding their heads, smiling and making me feel like church again. When I played the wrong note, they said, "That's alright, son." I felt like one of them then, as big as my grandpops and his men friends. When I finished, they all clapped and shook my hand. "Nice work, little man."

"We gonna need to pull up another chair soon," my grandpops told me. "But for now, you need to get on to bed."

My ma took me in and got me washed up. When I settled in, I laid awake listening to them play, thinking wasn't nothing better than my grandpops, Friday nights, and music.

THREE

Vicksburg, Mississippi 1941

My aunt Shirley told me I was gonna love learning my letters and numbers at school, but that wasn't what I liked best. First day of school, Grandpops drove me all the way to the schoolhouse in his truck. I was thinking it'd be one of those big brick buildings like I see in town, but it wasn't much bigger than our house with a lot of the paint chipped away. 'Long the way, we saw Little Leonard and Fuller walking, and Grandpops pulled over and picked them up too. I mostly only saw them in church at Sunday school, but those were the two I played with most. Once, out in back of the church after service, I wrestled with Fuller, and when we came back in, Ma slapped me on the back of my neck for dirtying up the knees of my church pants. Fuller laughed behind his hand, till his momma did the same to him. Fuller and his big brother, Little Leonard, got a mess of sisters and girl cousins. Their family takes up two whole rows of pews at Sunday service.

I'm 'bout the only one who don't have brothers or sisters, just Ma and Grandpops. My cousins Dee, Sis, and Flora are too big to play with. Never get a chance to play tag and hide-and-seek when I ain't at Sunday school or maybe when I go visiting with Ma. Most times I'm fine being by myself or sitting with Grand-pops. I like the quiet of it. But at school, having a field with balls to kick and rope for tug of war, I could have played all day. Sometimes, when we'd get going good, Teacher, Miss Stokes, called us in to go back to our desks before we started getting "too wild," she said. I didn't like sitting at long tables and hard benches copying the numbers and letters Miss Stokes wrote on the chalkboard half as much as I like playing outside in the schoolyard.

Every day, after that first day, Grandpops asked me, "How you doing with your letters?"

And every day I told him, "Fine." But truth was, when every-one was writing on their papers, I was looking out the window, just waiting to go on out and play. Miss Stokes said I wasn't trying hard enough, but every time I did, I'd get the letters all mixed up in my head. Sometimes she'd lean over me, smelling like cocoa butter and lemons, and put her hand, so smooth and dark brown, over mine to trace the letters on my paper. "There you go, Lymon," she'd say smiling. I thought she had to be the prettiest teacher there ever was, even though she was the only one I ever seen. With her next to me, felt like I could write every letter of the alphabet with my eyes closed, but soon as she walked away to help someone else, the letters would get mixed up again.

Just when the leaves were turning was when Grandpops started getting sick.

"Where's your grandpa?" Fuller asked me the second day I walked all the way to school with them.

"He ain't been feeling good," I told him.

Think they liked getting a ride in Grandpops' truck, but I liked the walking 'cause it meant I had more time with Little Leonard and Fuller. Half the time we raced each other till we were just 'bout out of breath. But soon as we saw the school bus coming down the road, taking the white kids to their school across town, we'd jump in the ditch to hide so we didn't get the dust from the wheels in our faces and have to hear the nasty words they yelled from the window. Only when it passed good, we'd throw rocks at the back of the bus, knowing we'd miss, but feeling good we did something. Sometimes we'd yell our own bad words, not so loud anyone could hear, then laugh till our sides just about bust.

When Grandpops hadn't gone to work for two weeks and wasn't getting any better, Ma started making less food, not even enough for second helpings. First, I thought it was 'cause Grandpops was barely eating, then I saw her counting coins out of her purse 'fore she went into town for groceries. Ma prayed half the night, begging God to "see us through." Didn't know if she meant the money, or Grandpops, or both. Was barely enough food for my lunch sack.

Now, every day I got home from school, Grandpops was sitting up in bed looking smaller and smaller. After the doctor came and looked Grandpops over good, Ma told me the doctor said it was his heart. But when I asked Grandpops how his heart was feeling, he told me, "Still pumping," and I thought that meant he was getting better.

When I came home from school, first thing I went straight to his room.

"There's my Lymon," he said, like he'd been waiting all day for me to come home.

"Look at this, Grandpops," I'd tell him, 'cause just 'bout every day I brought something home to make him feel better. Grandpops was always looking over the things I collected like I found buried treasure. So, I showed him the rock that looked like a star and a brown and white feather with fat stripes all the way down.

"Woowee, you got some finds today, didn't you," he said so quiet I had to lean in close. I put the feather in his hand. His skin felt dry as tree bark. The wiggly veins sticking up made his hand look like a map.

"What kind of feather you think this is?" I asked him.

He turned it over and looked close. "This here's an owl feather. Probably that one we hear making all that fuss outside your window all hours of the night." He smiled.

"When I get up from this bed, me and you gonna have to do some more feather hunting. But let me rest just a bit more now." Grandpops closed his eyes. When his breathing got heavy, I went out to the parlor and took out his guitar. Polished it up for him. It was a long time since he had his Friday night friends over to play.

Next day when I got home from school, I didn't have any

treasures, but Grandpops said, "Play a little something for me, son." I ran and got the guitar.

"I polished it for you," I told him.

"Can see that. You taking such good care of my baby, I'm gonna have to give it to you to take care of till I get back on my feet."

"Me?" I asked him.

"Yes you. Now let's see what you got."

I started in playing.

"Careful now with that chord," he'd said when I messed up. "The C sharp can be tricky."

Ma stopped fussing after me to do chores long as I was in with Grandpops. She let me sit hours by his bed, and never said one thing 'bout setting the table or taking out the trash. Seemed every day Grandpops talked less and less till he finally stopped talking at all. Even then, I'd sit by the bed, rubbing his hand. I even told him 'bout how pretty Miss Stokes was and the bad words I yelled at the white-people school bus. But nothing could made him talk.

Aunt Shirley came by every Sunday with her almost grown-up daughters, Sis and Flora, and I could hear them in the kitchen talking 'bout Grandpops and crying to Ma. Grandpops' Friday-night friends started coming 'round too, Mister Joe, Mister Bastion, and Mister Stroud. They stood at the foot of his bed, heads hung low. Heard Mister Joe singing one of Grandpops' favorite songs, not loud like he sang on Friday nights, but soft as a whisper, like he was telling Grandpops a secret.

FOUR

Vicksburg, Mississippi 1941

ONE day after school, Ma had me wait out on the porch while she brought in the basin of hot, soapy water to wash up Grandpops. It was finally cooling down some, and I was in the front yard flinging pebbles at an empty bottle of soda pop when I heard a car coming down the road.

I hadn't seen Aunt Vera and Uncle Clark since before my daddy went away. And even though their big gray car was covered in dust, Aunt Vera looked like a fancy movie star when she got out. She had a red scarf tied around her head and sunglasses and high heels women wear to church on Sunday mornings. I ran to the trunk to help with the suitcases, and she kissed me 'bout ten times.

"I can't believe how big you've gotten, Lymon," she said, and kissed me some more. Uncle Clark shook my hand hard.

First, I was just glad to see Aunt Vera, till I realized if she was home and it wasn't summertime, there must be something important going on. Right away Aunt Vera went in to see Grandpops. He wasn't talking anymore then, but you couldn't tell Aunt Vera that.

"Daddy, I'm here," she told Grandpops. "How you doing today, Daddy?"

I thought Ma should have told her that Grandpops couldn't answer. Uncle Clark got their things settled into her old room, and finally Aunt Vera left Grandpops' room, wiping her eyes. She changed into a flowery housecoat and went into the kitchen to help Ma with dinner. Uncle Clark sat out back smoking a cigarette while they talked.

'Fore long I heard Aunt Vera crying some more.

"Deliver him, God," she said over and over. "Deliver him."

"Hush now, Vera," I heard Ma tell her. "He can still hear you."

In the morning, Ma didn't wake me up like she usually did, but I could hear Aunt Vera crying and praying, and Uncle Clark saying, "It's gonna be all right, Vera." Didn't hear nothing from Ma. The door to Grandpops' room was open wide. Ma'd been keeping the curtain closed so the room stayed cool, but now the curtains were pushed away from the windows so it was bright as could be. Aunt Vera and Ma looked up as I walked in. Grandpops was lying still in the middle of the bed.

"He's gone on, Lymon," Aunt Vera said.

"Gone on to heaven?"

"Yes, Lord willing." Aunt Vera pulled me close.

They laid Grandpops out in the front room to wait for the funeral people to come and get him the next morning. I sat outside, missing supper, afraid to go in till Ma told me to come on and get washed up for bed. She let me hold her hand when I walked past Grandpops. That night after all the lights were out and the house was quiet, I lay in my bed wide awake, wanting to go out and make sure he was really gone, but too scared to do it. When I sat up, I heard Ma, moaning low. Sounded like her head was in her pillow.

Aunt Shirley brought me a shirt and hand-me-down suit, too long in the arms. I had to wear my old shoes, but Ma polished them up good.

"Your grandpop be proud to see you looking so strong and handsome," Aunt Shirley said. "Looking just like your daddy."

"Is he coming?" I asked her.

"Is who coming, baby?" she said.

"My daddy."

She put her head down and fussed with the collar on my shirt. "Your daddy can't come just yet, but we need you to be a little man for today."

I nodded, and I didn't say my daddy was a real grown man, not a boy like me dressed like one.

I still waited for Daddy to come, all the way till we got in the car to go to the church.

———◆———

People I never seen before shook my hand. Told me, "He's gone on to a better place" and "You take care of your grandma now, hear?" Felt like they were talking to someone else. Ma hit my arm to tell me it was time to walk up front with her one last time, 'fore they laid him down. I walked as slow as I could till I was the last in line. Looking at Grandpops in his best suit and tie he wore to other folks' funerals, I stood there just wishing I could hear his voice one more time.

When no one was looking, I reached in my pocket and pulled out the owl feather I brought and put it on top of his dry hand 'fore they closed the box he was laying in.

FIVE

Milwaukee, Wisconsin 1942

AFTER Grandpops passed, Aunt Vera, Uncle Clark, and Aunt Shirley had a meeting, sitting 'round the kitchen table with Ma. I stood close outside the room so I could hear.

"Ma, me and Clark think you and Lymon should come on up to Milwaukee with us," Aunt Vera told her.

"We ain't going nowhere," Ma said. I could hear the mad in her voice but a little bit of scared too. "I'm gonna stay right here."

"Ma, we barely had enough to put Daddy in the ground. There just ain't enough…" Aunt Vera said.

"I'll stay with Shirley." I didn't hear nothing from Aunt Shirley but a long breath, like she was tired. "Ma, you know I ain't got the room for both of y'all."

I heard Ma push her chair back and I had to run into my room so she couldn't tell I was listening.

After that, it felt like Ma was dying slow just like Grandpops. She stopped speaking and wouldn't eat her supper.

"Can I go outside?" I'd ask her, just to get her to talk, but she pretended she didn't hear a word.

Aunt Vera told me, "Don't mind her, Lymon. She'll come around soon enough."

And one night she did. Ma was in the kitchen washing dishes, when Aunt Shirley came by. She went into the room with Aunt Vera and the two of them whispered for a long time. They came out together and walked into the kitchen. I stood quiet outside the door, listening. Aunt Vera said, "Ma...we gotta talk." But instead of Ma answering, I heard a pot bang in the sink.

Just when I thought they were gonna get tired of waiting for Ma to say something, Aunt Shirley tried again. "We're gonna help you pack up all your things, Ma. I think you're gonna like Milwaukee. Vera and Clark..." Ma didn't stop washing the dishes.

"How you know what I'm gonna like?" Ma said.

I put my hand over my mouth 'cause I almost made a sound.

"Milwaukee's a real pretty city, Ma," Aunt Vera said. "And my pastor, Reverend Lawson at Calvary..."

"I ain't going," Ma said.

It was quiet again.

"Ma...we told you—" Aunt Vera started soft and slow.

"And I told you," Ma said, mean as I ever heard her. "We'll make out fine here. First I lose Frank, and then I gotta lose my home?"

Aunt Vera ran out the room crying so fast she didn't see me standing near the door.

I waited to see if Aunt Shirley was coming out too, but then I heard her talking again. "Ma, you ain't got no choice. Daddy would want us to see you and Lymon were looked after. This is the way it's gotta be." Aunt Shirley walked straight out the house and I heard her start her car.

Even though the water was still running from the faucet, I could hear Ma crying, "Lord, Lord…"

————•————

After that, Ma seemed too tired to fight with Aunt Vera or Aunt Shirley. I didn't hear any more crying or moaning at night, just quiet. 'Specially when she started packing up all our clothes into four beat-up suitcases. Don't think she said more than two words in the car, all the way to Milwaukee.

————•————

Wasn't so much that I was looking forward to going to school in Milwaukee, but I spent the whole summer watching Ma get meaner and meaner. To me, Aunt Vera, to just 'bout everybody. And I wasn't used to having to live with so many people. My cousin Dee and her husband were living there with their baby. I slept in one room with Ma, and they slept in the room next door, but their baby, Essie, cried all night long. Milwaukee wasn't as quiet as Vicksburg, but I had to go outside just to hear myself think. Most times I played in back by myself on the worn-out patches of grass, digging up ants and worms or playing soldier, sometimes just trying to remember the songs Grandpops taught me on the guitar. When we left Vicksburg, we could barely fit all the suitcases in the car, and then Uncle Clark told me, "We don't have room for that guitar, son."

Ma spoke loud then.

"We'll make room," she told him. Uncle Clark squeezed it in the last spot he could find.

Right before school was starting, we moved from Aunt Vera's onto Lloyd Street. Miss Dot lived next door with her son Lenny, but he was old too. A man with a cane lived across the street. Some of the houses were empty, and one house looked like a house but it was really a church. We could hear the whooping and shouting every Sunday morning and sometimes in the middle of the week when Ma said they were having Bible study. "Ain't a need for all that shouting when you learning the Word," she said sucking her teeth. When Ma wasn't looking, I threw up my hands and made like I got the spirit too.

———————

Aunt Vera signed me up for my new school at Fourth Street Elementary in Milwaukee. I tried not to get too sad thinking about how on my last first day of school, I sat with Grandpops in his truck, now I was walking with just me and Ma. I think Ma was trying not to think about it too 'cause she let me wear my best shirt and the pants from the suit I wore to Grandpops' funeral. She got up early and made me more eggs and bacon than I could eat. She could walk pretty good then, but we left early so she could take her time. I was in a hurry, hoping I'd finally meet some boys in Milwaukee. I walked so fast, I had to keep turning 'round to come back for her. She told me more than once to "slow down."

Even though she left early, Ma walked so slow we got there same time as everyone else. Everyone came walking with their mommas or daddies, sometimes both, but not a one that I could see came with their grandma. That's when I slowed down. The girls were in dresses and the boys dressed as nice as church Sundays.

This school looked like the picture in my head. Big and brick with steps in the front. Made me stop to take it all in.

"What you waiting for?" Ma said too loud when I stopped walking. "Go on ahead."

I saw some of them turn and look at me and look at Ma and her swolled legs and raggedy dress. I had to hold her hand to go up the stairs, and by the time we got to the door we were the last to go in.

"I'll go by myself, Ma," I said. Hoping maybe some of the others didn't see me with my grandma.

"I come all this way, now you want me to go home? Let's get on to the class." We walked down a long hallway to room 114 till we saw a tall white teacher waiting at the door.

"Good morning," she said to Ma. "Welcome to Fourth Street Elementary." She was young and pretty, with her two front teeth sticking out far like a rabbit, but nowhere near as pretty as Miss Stokes. "I'm Miss Arthur. And what is your name?" she bent low to ask me.

"That's Lymon," Ma said, 'fore I could even answer. "He gets fidgety, but if he acts up, you let me know."

"I'm sure we won't have any problems, right, Lymon?" she said smiling.

"Yes ma'am."

"Say goodbye to your…mother?"

"I'm his grandma," Ma said.

"Oh? Will I be meeting his parents?"

"No, you will not," Ma said. "Like I said, if he don't mind you, let me know." Ma nodded at me, and Miss Arthur told me to go in and find a seat.

I walked into a room with windows across one whole wall. There wasn't a potbellied stove in the corner for heat like at my old school, just a big ole radiator in the corner. Didn't take long for me to find some boys to sit with. All the girls with their pretty dresses and bows sat on one side. Every one of them dressed fancy, with their hair pressed and shiny with Sweet Georgia Brown pomade like it was Easter Sunday, sat up front near the teacher's desk. Could tell here I wasn't going to find anyone like Little Leonard and Fuller. I tucked my scuffed shoes under my seat. One of the boys sitting close to me asked, "That's your momma who brought you?"

"Nah," I said. "That's my ma."

"So that is your momma?"

"No, that's my grandma."

"Why do you call her Ma?"

Said I didn't know, just what I called her.

"She looked old."

One boy asked, "Where's your real Ma?"

I moved away and found another seat. Miss Arthur walked in and looked as white as cotton in a room filled up with brown faces. She gave us pencils and paper and Miss Arthur told us to first write our names at the top and copy the words from the chalkboard. She walked up and down the rows looking from side to side at our papers, saying, "Nice work" and "Beautiful penmanship," but when she got to me, she stopped.

"Take your time, Lymon," she said. "We do our *best* work in this class." The boy behind me laughed soft. I moved my arm on top of my desk, half covering my paper, so no one could see my big, wobbly letters. I didn't have Miss Stokes to put her hand over mine and help me, and when I thought about her, I pressed down hard and broke my pencil.

When I left in the morning, I could barely wait to get to school, but between Ma and the questions, the fancy dresses and the boys in their shirts and ties, my wobbly letters and broken pencil, all I wanted to do now was go home.

School never did get much better after the first day. Nice as Miss Arthur was, she wasn't Little Leonard or Fuller or even Miss Stokes. Out on the playground, sometimes I joined in with the other boys playing tag or kickball, but when it came time to walk home, seemed like everybody went to one part of town and I went to another. Even though I was never 'shamed about having a daddy at Parchman, I was 'shamed now 'bout Ma and her swolled legs and not having any people in Milwaukee 'sides her and Aunt Vera's family. In Vicksburg, it felt like just 'bout everybody was family. And if they weren't, they knew the type of people I was from.

In class, I worked on my letters, nice and slow, like Miss Arthur told me, but they didn't look nothing like the other boys' letters. Most times, when we finished lessons, I turned over my paper, hoping no one would see I was still writing like a baby. Seemed like I was playing a game of Mother May I? where I took one baby step while everybody else in class took five.

SIX

Milwaukee, Wisconsin 1942

WHEN we first got to Milwaukee and I walked with Aunt Vera into town for groceries, I thought there was so many colored folks up North you wouldn't hardly know you weren't in Mississippi. Running straight through the center of town is a street colored folks call Chocolate Avenue. And that's not 'cause there's a sweet shop selling candy. It's 'cause there's colored folks all up and down Walnut Street. Colored folks here ain't got to go ask the white folks to buy nothing from their stores 'cause they got their own stores for everything you need, and even things you don't. There were stores selling fruit and vegetables in stands out front, two restaurants, funeral parlors, a pool hall, three churches, the Columbia Savings and Loan bank, and a place that sold ice. We passed by a building with a picture of a big white tooth, and Aunt Vera told me that was Dr. Roberts' office.

"Why do you need a doctor for your teeth?" I asked her.

"Sometimes they get to aching and they need to be pulled. That's what the dentist does."

Just like Vicksburg, Milwaukee's like two towns in one. North Side for colored folks and South side for whites. Aunt Vera told me it wasn't safe for a colored boy to step foot out of the North Side, but with all that was going on here, I didn't know why I would. A lot of the streets here had numbers for names and the town was laid out like one big puzzle.

Aunt Vera let me take my time staring at the traffic lights flashing red and green, and 'specially the streetcar.

"I looked just like you when I first saw those streetcars." She laughed. "I wrote Ma and Daddy that in the North they have trains riding through the middle of town, and they must have thought I had lost my natural mind."

That summer, I had every day to myself. If Aunt Vera worked third shift, she'd come by in her big car and take me over to Lapham pool in the morning. She'd beep the horn twice but never came in. Ma would suck her teeth when she heard the beep, but she didn't say nothing more when I ran out the house.

I couldn't swim, but I liked splashing in the end where I could stand. Aunt Vera, and sometimes my cousin Dee and her baby, would come with their bathing suits and sunglasses, and let their legs hang in the water while I was in the pool. Those were the days I'd miss the boys back home. We never had a pool in Vicksburg, but I know we would have had some fun riding piggyback and dunking our heads in the ice-cold water. When Aunt Vera took me to her church picnic, I met a boy my age named Calvin and in between eating potato salad and hot dogs and the cold chicken Aunt Vera brought, we played like I did in Vicksburg. But he was just in Milwaukee visiting his grandma, so I didn't see him again. Now I go to town every chance I get. First, I went just to Apex Cab to give Mr. Kirby the numbers Ma writes on a piece of paper. Ma's never won any money with the numbers, but she puts together a little money each week to play. Sometimes I wonder what she'd do with all the money if she hits, but I didn't think on it too hard, 'cause so far, she never even came close. Sometimes, I'd find reasons to go into town. Tell Ma I was heading over to Aunt Vera's, when all I wanted was to watch the streetcar and walk down streets looking in the stores. Milwaukee sounded like a record, playing all kinds of sounds at once. When I walked along the street, I could hear the sewing machines from Ideal's Tailor Shop, the clicking of the hot combs in the beauty shops, and the bell from Tankar's filling station when gas was pumping. But if I was in town after supper, sometimes I heard real music too coming from The Flame club. The door was closed, but through the window, cracked open in front, I could hear bands warming up their instruments. I'd just lean up against the side of the building and try to remember Grandpops and his Friday-night friends. If Mr. Bunky came out though, I had to keep walking.

"You ain't got nothing better to do than hang around my place of business?" Sounded like he was asking but he was really telling. I didn't wait to give him an answer.

Milwaukee was a whole lot different than Vicksburg, but

what made me want to stay, what made me love that city, were the days, standing outside The Flame, when I could hear the musicians playing. Even if Mr. Bunky chased me away, I'd go on home, take out Grandpops' guitar, and play everything I'd heard. And no matter what day of the week it was, I'd pretend it was Friday night.

SEVEN

Milwaukee, Wisconsin 1943

WHEN I next saw my daddy, the rain had finally stopped
and the warm was making its way back into most days. This time
Daddy wasn't wearing striped pajamas, but a clean white shirt,
black pants, and black shoes. He walked all the way from the
bus depot in town, carrying his clothes in a brown-paper sack,
and stepped into the house smiling. He hugged Ma and me, but
when he looked around and Grandpops wasn't there to shake
his hand, he stopped smiling.

"Sorry I couldn't be here, Ma," he said, with a catch in his
throat.

I thought Ma would have held him then, seeing how bad he
felt 'bout missing Grandpops' funeral while he was at Parchman
Farm, but she didn't. She just let him stand there feeling bad
about himself. I hugged him 'round his waist though. Felt good
to have a daddy again that I could see every day.

He stayed a long time then. He helped Ma 'round the house
cleaning, fixing every broken-down thing he could get his hands
on till Ma told him, "You got to get on outta my way!"

But when Daddy wasn't getting in Ma's way, he took me out back and taught me new songs on Grandpops' guitar, and in between we talked.

"I made a lot of mistakes, Lymon, but you about the one thing I did right," he said one day, looking down at me.

"What kind of mistakes?" I asked, trying to figure out my fingering on the strings.

"Kind of mistakes lands a man in a place like Parchman Farm kind of mistakes," he said.

Ma already told me not to talk about that place in her house. But my daddy was home now. And he looked like he was in the mood for talking, and I was in the mood for asking. I looked back through the screen door to make sure Ma wasn't in the kitchen listening.

"You a farmer?" I whispered. I was sitting on a piece of grass out in the yard, digging for worms, while Daddy was on the front porch trying to fix one of the steps that rotted in the middle. Ma told me to leave Daddy be, but I followed him everywhere he went, afraid if he left, I'd never see him again.

I knew all about farming from the folks in Vicksburg who picked cotton and tobacco. Back there, Ma had a plot out back for vegetables, one in front for flowers.

"You know I ain't no farmer," Daddy told me.

"Then why'd you live on a farm in Parchman?" I asked.

Daddy took a good, long breath and sat down. I came over and sat down next to him.

"You ever do something Ma and Grandpops tell you you not supposed to do?" he asked.

"Sometimes," I said, feeling 'shamed.

"What happens then? When you do something you shouldn't be doing?"

"Grandpops used to yell, but Ma gives me a whipping," I told him.

Daddy laughed. "They used to do the same thing to me when I was your age. Truth is, Lymon, I went and did something bad, and the law gave me a whipping by sending me to Parchman."

"Why'd they send you to a farm 'cause you did something bad?"

We could hear Ma moving 'round in the kitchen getting supper started, and Daddy quieted his voice.

"Parchman ain't no farm, Lymon. It's a prison. But mainly just free labor for rich white folks. They had us picking cotton from morning till night. They say old Abe Lincoln freed the slaves, but they alive and well at Parchman." Daddy shook his head.

"Did you steal something?" I asked him.

"No son. Worse than that. I hurt someone."

"Hurt him bad?" I asked.

"Bad enough to land me in Parchman for assault."

"Is the man dead?"

Daddy put his head down, poking at the nails popped loose in the step. "No, he's not dead."

I put my hand on his back. "Did you say you was sorry?"

"Said I was sorry to the police, the lawyer, the judge, and anybody else who'd listen. But sometimes when you do something bad, you just got to pay the price."

Daddy was quiet then. Then I heard him sniffling. When he looked at me his eyes were full of water.

Now I couldn't stop asking questions. "Was he your friend?"

"I knew him from 'round the way. Can't say we were *friends*, but *friendly*. All that changes when folks get to drinking and such. Can't even remember now what we were fighting about," Daddy said. "I'm sorry for leaving you behind like I did. You must think I'm a sad excuse for a daddy."

I didn't know how to answer. Sitting next to Daddy made me forget all those years of waiting, not knowing when he was gonna be home.

"You're here now," I said.

"Yeah," he said, smiling again. "I'm here now."

I checked again to make sure Ma couldn't hear us talking. "What was it like in there?" I whispered.

"Bad. Real bad, son. Not fit for an animal. Let alone a man."

"But it looked real nice when we came to visit," I said, remembering how we spread out my blanket and ate Ma's good food, and how folks laughed and danced.

"That ain't the real Parchman. That's the visiting-day Parchman!" Daddy ain't never talked to me mean like Ma does, but he did then.

I stopped my asking then 'cause if Ma heard all that fussing and Parchman talk, I'd be sure to get a whipping. The day was going so good with Daddy, I was hoping it'd stay that way.

Daddy smiled again. "Looks like you had to be the man around here when I couldn't," he said to me.

"Yessir," I said, though I don't know what was being a man 'bout going to school and doing the chores Ma yelled at me to do.

"I know you only, what seven or eight years old now? But Ma was counting on you, son, with me and Pops gone."

"I'm eight years old," I told Daddy, feeling like seven was just a baby. "Aunt Vera brought me a cake."

"That's right, eight," Daddy said smiling. Now that he was smiling again, I had to ask one more question.

"But you're back now, right?"

Daddy didn't say nothing.

"Daddy?" I looked up.

"Thinking about getting on, son. Got a gig with a friend of mine for a bit then I'll need to see what else I can find. It'll give me a couple of dollars in my pocket. Been a while since I was paid for an honest day's work."

"You gonna leave me with Ma?"

"Just till I get on my feet, son. Then it's gonna be me and you, I promise you that."

"How long is that gonna be? You getting your feet?"

"Getting *on* my feet." He laughed. "Be a little bit. But soon."

"Can I come with you now?" I asked.

"Nah, Lymon. This ain't no kind of job for you to be on."

All of sudden, I could feel myself getting mad and sad at the same time.

"Does Ma know you're leaving?"

"Getting ready to tell her now."

I've never been 'shamed of my daddy, but back when Daddy went away, 'fore I even knew what Parchman was, Ma and Grandpops told me my daddy was gonna be gone for a while. Never said why and never said where. Then after we visited, Ma told me, "You just keep quiet about visiting your daddy, you hear me? We don't need folks in our business."

"What business?" I asked her.

"Our dirty laundry," Ma said mad. That night, when Grandpops put me to bed, he said to me, "Now, Lymon, folks ask you questions about your daddy, you just tell them they can ask me or your ma anything they want to know."

"You mean 'bout the dirty laundry?" I asked him.

Grandpops tucked up my blanket. "Yeah, the dirty laundry. Your daddy's gonna be home before you know it," he said. But in the dark, Grandpops sounded like I did when I was trying not to cry.

"You okay, Grandpops?"

"I'll be just fine," he told me. "And so will you."

But soon enough, he wasn't fine. And he never was again.

"Last time I saw Pops was in that place." My daddy started

up again, looking off into the road. "I promised Pops I'd make things right soon as I got home. Be a son he could be proud of. He said to me, ''Course you will, son.' And here I am, no better off than when I left."

I couldn't look at my daddy so sad. "I'll go help Ma with supper," I told him.

I stood up but he didn't move. Just kept staring out ahead. I closed the screen door behind me. And when supper was ready and I came to get him, my daddy hadn't even moved.

———————◆·◆———————

A few days later, Daddy rubbed my head goodbye and left promising he'd be back soon. Days passed, then weeks, and as it was getting good and hot outside, I went back to almost forgetting what it felt like to have my daddy home with me.

EIGHT

Milwaukee, Wisconsin 1943

MA says Daddy comes when the winds change and that seems 'bout right. When the leaves turn red and yellow, or flowers start growing, or when the radiator starts spitting out steam is when I know I'll see him.

Most times I hear him 'fore I see him. Car door slams and I can hear his loud laugh in the night with folks he met 'long the way, who gave him a ride. Sometimes I hear the gravelly sound of his singing coming from down the street, but it's always me hears him first.

Tonight, from the bed in the room I share with Ma, I hear him whistling the song he taught me on the guitar last time he was in town. I pull on my pants and run to the door.

"Stop running in the house, boy!" Ma yells, sleep in her voice. I can hear the wheeze in the back of her throat. She yells some more, she's gonna need me to get her medicine. I got good at pretending I don't hear nothing she says. I got one ear listening for her in the back room, making sure she don't get up, and one ear waiting to hear how close Daddy is. Can tell by her hard breathing she's sitting up now in bed, trying to see what I'm up to. When I hear his boots on the porch and his whistling is right outside the door, I open it 'fore he can even knock.

He stops his whistling short and smiles with all his teeth. He looks even tireder than the last time I seen him. Got a beard growing scraggly.

"Come here, boy," he says, pulling me in.

My daddy ain't a tall man, but last time I seen him, my head was just at his chest. Now it's just a little bit higher.

"You steady growing! Ma must be feeding you good!" He laughs, stepping inside, rubbing my head as he comes in out of the chill.

"Who's that you talking to?" Ma yells from the bedroom.

"It's the boogeyman, Ma! Who you think it is?"

Ma don't say nothing. All we hear is her wheezing.

"Lemme go on back a minute," Daddy says. I follow 'long behind, but he puts his hand out to stop me. I go into the kitchen instead, walking through the front room. When we moved here, going on three years now, Aunt Vera gave us some of her hand-me-down furniture. Calvary Baptist down the street gave us the rest. But the house is still mostly empty except for the old flowered couch, beat-up rug, and two tables on either end, one brown, one black. Grandpops' guitar is sitting in the corner. I grab that and bring it in the kitchen. I see if I can get something together for Daddy to eat. The pot of greens and ham hocks from dinner is still sitting on the stove along with the last of the cornbread. I go looking for a plate in the sink full of dirty dishes. Wash that off good and set it on the table.

Daddy closes the door to Ma's bedroom, and I can hear Daddy talking, Ma yelling. Daddy talking some more. Ma yells louder. Seems like her wheezing would make her quiet down some, but it don't. The door opens to Ma shouting "...ain't no hotel..." and Daddy closes it quick, comes straight into the kitchen. He sits down heavy.

"See Ma's mouth ain't slowing down none." He laughs. "What y'all got in here to eat?" he asks, lighting a cigarette.

"Ma don't like no one smoking in the house," I remind him, opening the back door to let the smoke out.

He puts a finger to his lips. "Then let's make it our secret." Daddy tilts his head all the way back and takes a long puff.

I sit down across from him. Together we stay quiet as can be, him puffing and looking at the ceiling like he's looking in a mirror. Me watching him puff. When he stubs his cigarette on the bottom of his boot, I hand him the plate of greens and cornbread and a spoon.

Daddy talks with his mouth full of food, barely stopping to swallow.

"Last town, we barely played one set when some crackers pulled up in a truck." Daddy whistled through his teeth. "We took out of there so fast, almost left my shadow behind."

"You like being on the road all the time?" I asked him.

"We spend more time trying to avoid the po-lice and the

sundown towns than we do on stage." Daddy smiled, tired. "But ain't nothing quite like making music. You know something about that, right?" Daddy rubbed my head.

"What happens if the police catch you?" I asked him.

"First off, police ain't gonna catch up to me. Second, long as we're passing through those white towns 'fore sundown like the law wants, we're good. And third"—Daddy held up three fingers—"Parchman ain't never gonna see me again."

Daddy lit up another cigarette and shook his head like there was water in his ears.

"Why you got me talking about this mess? How's your Aunt Vera, Uncle Clark?" he asks me.

"Good, but I don't see them much since Aunt Vera started working over in Falk Foundry with Uncle Clark. And Dee just had 'nother baby so they been busy."

Daddy nods his head slow.

"How's Ma treating you?" he finally asks.

"Same, I guess. Ma is Ma," I tell him. "Her leg's been getting worse, so she's in the bed more. Can't get up and around like she used to."

"Doctor been here?"

I put my head down. "Ma says we can't afford no doctor coming 'round here all the time. So, she has me cleaning it in the morning and at night. She has a salve I rub on too. Smells nasty."

Daddy laughs big.

"Vera needs to help you. I'll see her on my way out."

"Daddy, don't say nothing to Aunt Vera. Ma'll get mad if she thinks I said something. Said she don't want Aunt Vera in her business. With what Aunt Vera gives, we got enough to get by."

"Ma is Ma, huh," he said.

"What you mean, way out? Thought you were staying for a bit," I ask him.

"Not this time, son. Got a gig over in Greene County next week and I gotta start making my way there. That reminds me."

Daddy pulls a case from his pocket. Takes out his A harmonica, the one he plays on with his band, then wipes it clean with a cloth. The words MARINE BAND on the side are almost worn clean.

"Listen to this." He plays a song slow and long, sounds like a woman crying. Daddy bows his head and closes his eyes while he plays, like he's praying to God. I wonder what kind of sad he's thinking to make music sound like that.

"That sounds good," I tell him. "Real good." He laughs and hits me on the back. I pick up Grandpops' guitar I brought into the kitchen. "Can you show me?" Daddy pulls his chair 'longside mine and shows me where to put my fingers and starts strumming. His fingers are ashy white 'round his knuckles and cracked 'round his nails. But we both got the same long, skinny fingers. My grandpops used to tell me I had "piano playing hands" just like my daddy. I ain't never touched a piano, but I plan to one day.

After watching Daddy for a bit, I try out the chords until I get it just about right, then Daddy joins in on his harmonica.

Here in the kitchen making music, without Ma fussing, starts me with that wanting feeling I get sometimes. For a real momma, not a grandma I call Ma. And a house with me and my parents, all living together, making music, and feeling like family.

NINE

Milwaukee, Wisconsin 1943

AFTER Daddy finished up his plate of food, I could see he was getting tired again.

He stood up and piled his plate with the others in the sink.

"Daddy," I asked, "you ever hear from my momma?"

He looked at me hard. His eyes were red and watery. He lit another cigarette. Took a little bottle out of his jacket pocket and took a long sip.

"I hear she's still living over in Chicago," he said.

"How far away is Chicago?" I asked him.

"What, you writing a book?" He tried to laugh and stood up, but I grabbed his hand.

"Tell me again how you met my momma," I said.

"I told you all this before, Lymon," he said. "I'm gonna sound like a broken record."

I didn't let his hand go, and he sat back down. "You gonna let me close my eyes after I tell it, right?"

"Yessir," I said.

Daddy had to talk low 'cause we didn't want to wake up Ma.

I sat close, listening. Daddy's voice always sound bigger than he was. Big and low and gravelly, like he should be seven feet tall instead small and skinny like he is.

"First time I saw your momma was at a dance. She was in a flowered dress with a white flower in her hair, dancing with her cousin. I was playing in the band, at that little spot down by Harmon's place near the lake, and I was out in front, so I could see everything. It was dark in there, but watching your momma dance was like someone had turned on a light. I smiled at her best as I could when I wasn't playing, but she was too busy dancing to even notice. On my break, I went over and asked her name. She kinda rolled her eyes at me.

"She said, real sweet, 'Daisy.'

"I was trying to be smooth, so I said, 'Like the flower?' and winked at her.

"'Just like it,' she told me, laughing with those pretty teeth. Her eyes were so little they almost looked closed. Like I said, it was dark in there, but I swear, she was about the prettiest thing I'd seen in a long time. I told the boys in the band to gimme a few minutes and I put my harmonica in my pocket and took her out to the dance floor. I did my best out there, but I could barely keep up!"

I stopped his story. "Were you a good dancer?" I asked.

"I could always keep time, but I didn't have nothing on your momma." He laughed.

"She must have appreciated me trying, 'cause she told me

where she lived. Told me I could stop by and call on her. So, the next day, I borrowed Grandpops' truck and made my way over there."

Even though I knew the story, I stopped him again. "Was she surprised to see you?"

"Let's just say, she didn't close the door in my face." Daddy poked me in my side. Even though Daddy told me he was tired, when he started talking 'bout how he met my momma, he looked wide awake now.

"I should have known your momma wasn't the kind of girl Ma and Grandpops be happy about me seeing. She was young, only fifteen, and her people, well they had a bit of a bad name. Wasn't her fault her folks spent their time drinking and fighting. I could tell, even young as she was, she wanted something better for herself. So, I kept her a secret for as long as I could. But once she started coming 'round with me to my gigs, word got back to them."

"And they were mad?" I asked.

"Mad ain't the word. But not near as mad as when I told them she was expecting you. Your grandpops sat me down and said, 'I thought you knew better, son. That girl's barely a woman herself. What you all gonna do with a baby?'

"I thought I was a man, and I told your grandpops, 'We'll figure it out, Pops.' I meant it too. Didn't think nothing else mattered long as we were in love."

"Were you gonna get married?" I asked.

"Now you gonna let me tell the story or keep asking questions?" Daddy said. "Your momma wanted a big wedding. Said she was gonna plan it right. But your grandpops didn't lie. We were just too young and dumb. When I quit school to work with him down at the mill, he could barely look at me. He was hoping I'd follow in Vera and Shirley's footsteps, graduate from high school, maybe even go to the trade school over in Jackson. But now that I had a mouth to feed, that wasn't something I could do." Daddy looked like telling this part hurt bad. "Vera and Shirley were long gone out the house then, married, starting their own families. I felt like with all that extra room, me and your momma could live there, just till we got settled in our own place. But you know Ma. She said ain't no way I was going to lie down in her house with any woman not my wife, even if she *was* carrying her grandbaby. Well that was just fine with me, so I went and stayed at her parents' place over in Waltersville. But being there never sat right with me. First off, they were so loud they made Ma seem quiet. Drinking and fussing all hours of the night. I didn't want any child of mine in that house. So, after you were born, I started bringing your momma by the house, hoping Ma and Grandpops see you, maybe they'd change their mind. Well, it worked. Partways at least. They took to you, but not to her."

"Was I a cute baby?"

"Not at first. You looked like a wrinkled-up ham hock when you were born. Took a while, but you finally got your daddy's good looks." We both laughed 'cause we both knew I didn't look nothing like my daddy.

"She knew Ma didn't care for her. She told me once, 'They think I ain't no kind of momma.'"

I laughed at Daddy's girl voice.

"I told her to give them some time to come around, but truth was, she couldn't be a momma to you when she still needed a momma herself. Seeing how much my folks took to you, she started leaving you with Ma and Grandpops, and before I knew it, I started hearing about her back dancing all hours of the night."

Daddy stopped again like it hurt.

"That's when the fighting started. And she started coming 'round less and less. But I made sure you were at the house with Ma when me and Grandpops went to work at the mill. I kept thinking if she had help, she'd get the hang of being a momma. But the less she came 'round, the madder Ma got."

Now Daddy made his voice sound just like Ma's.

"'What kind of momma don't keep their baby with them at night?' she'd say to Pops. When we worked late at the mill, and your momma didn't come to pick you up one time too many, Ma made up a little bed in a bureau drawer and you slept there most nights. When you got too big, Grandpops pulled out my old crib from the shed in back and fixed it up with a fresh coat of paint and put it in Aunt Vera and Aunt Shirley's old room. Woowee, you had a set of lungs on you. They could hear you crying next county over. But your grandpops knew what to do. Soon as you'd start to fussin,' he'd take out his guitar, start playing, and you'd fall right to sleep.

"When I heard your momma been seen around with Orvis Hall, I went to my daddy for some man-to-man advice. He was thinking on it, when I heard Ma at the screen door. You know how she don't miss a thing.

"'When you lie down with dogs, you wake up with fleas,' she told me. Now you know I love Ma, but I hated her then. I took off out the house, mad. Didn't come back for days. After that, I didn't see your momma much. 'Cept this one time when she came by the house and asked Ma if she could take you to see her people. Ma told me your momma was already big with Orvis's baby and looked so pitiful. She had a load of washing ahead of her to do so she told her to go on, just have me back by supper. But when supper came and went, and we got home from work, Ma told Grandpops to start up the truck, and we all marched right over to your momma's house. There was a house full of people, but there you were sitting alone on the porch crying. I didn't even have time to open the door to the truck before Ma was out, up those stairs, snatching you up so fast, your momma didn't have a chance to say much.

"She had the nerve to say to Ma, 'I was just getting ready to bring him back, right, Lymon?' pinching your cheek like you all were bosom buddies. Ma got you in the car and said, 'All that woman knows is how to talk foolishness.'

"When she got you home, Ma gave you a long hot bath in the tub, and I could hear her telling Pops she needed to scrub off the filth from that nasty house."

I knew the rest of the story too. The part Daddy didn't want to tell. That after that, I didn't see my momma much. Guess with the new baby coming, she forgot all about the old baby. Me. Only Ma I ever really knew was my daddy's Ma. My grandma.

———— · ————

Sometimes though when I think about my ma's garden back in Vicksburg, and the flowers lined up there all in a row, I think about my daddy and my momma's flower dress and the flower in her hair and a momma I don't hardly know named Daisy.

Daddy sat back on the couch cushions, tired again.

"Can we go to Chicago to see my momma?" I asked.

Daddy whistled out his teeth. "What's got into you tonight boy? You trying to keep me up all night?"

I asked the question I been scared to ask. "You think she wants to see me?"

"'Course she wants to see you," Daddy said.

"Then can we go?" I asked again.

Daddy always told me he'd been blessed with a daddy who never lied to him. Would look him straight in the eye and tell him what needed to be said, no matter how bad it hurt. Said he aimed to be the same kind of daddy to me.

"Don't work like that, Lymon," he said. "Your momma got a whole other life now."

I put my head down.

"Listen here." He pulled my head up so I could look him in the eye. "Let's talk about this in the morning. I can't barely keep my eyes open."

I opened the door to the bedroom quiet where Ma was sleeping and took the quilt off of my bed. Time I got back to the front room, he was stretched out on the couch in his clothes sleeping. I took off his boots and covered him with the quilt, tucking it up around his neck.

TEN

Milwaukee, Wisconsin 1943

WHEN I woke the next morning, I could tell by the sun coming in it was time to get up for school and could tell if I didn't get a move on, I was going to be late. Ma was still sleeping good. I hurried out to the front room. The quilt I gave Daddy was folded up neat in a square at the end of the couch.

"Daddy!" I called out, not caring if I woke up Ma. I looked in the kitchen, then the bathroom, but Daddy was gone.

Even though I was gonna be late for school, I didn't hurry. I put away the quilt, then brushed my teeth.

I didn't say goodbye to Ma when I left out. When I finally walked in the classroom, teacher said, "Lymon, how nice of you to join us this morning." I didn't turn, just kept walking to the back to my seat.

"I said, how nice of you to join us this morning," she said again. "Is there anything you'd like to say to the class?" she asked, walking toward me.

"Ma'am?" I asked.

"How about we start with an apology for being late." She smiled. That same smile she gave when she asked me about figuring a problem on the board. I could hear the girls in the front row whispering. The rest of the class was quiet.

I looked at her. At her pasty-white face and red hair. Her fat neck was poked out over a pearl necklace and she had red lipstick on her teeth.

"I'm waiting," she said, like she was singing a song.

She had on a dress with big yellow flowers, made me think of the couch at home. And the folded-up quilt Daddy left at the end of it.

"I ain't apologizing for nothing," I said to her.

She looked like I slapped her. Her face got all red.

"Get to the principal's office right now!" she screamed.

I stood up, walked back up the aisle, past the whispering girls in front, and straight out the classroom door.

Instead of turning left out the door and walking to the principal's office, I turned right to the side door. The hallway was empty, the floors smooth and shiny like they just been polished. I walked down the stairs to the door and out to the school parking lot. Back in Mississippi, Grandpops used to make sure I got to school, but after he passed, and Ma got sick, seemed like her sickness was all that mattered. Wasn't that she didn't want me going to school, but Ma and her sickness come before anything else. Even before my schooling.

I walked down Fourth Street, then turned onto Walnut. The thing I liked best about Milwaukee was all the streetcars. On the corner of Third and Walnut streets I stopped and sat on the curb in front of Goldberg's Pharmacy, watching men getting off their shift at the foundry. When the streetcar stopped, some women got off, laughing loud. Their white dresses were still clean after a day of cooking and keeping house for their white folks. Everybody looked a lot happier coming home from work than they did going. Listening to the streetcar clang by reminded me of the train we took to visit Daddy at Parchman, my only time on a train. Even when Ma told me that train ride was too long and Daddy would be home "soon enough," I still asked Grandpops just 'bout every week when we were going back. But when he got sick, I stopped asking. After he passed, and we moved in with Aunt Vera and her family, I asked Ma, "How's my daddy going to find us here?"

"Vera sent word," she told me. But then one year passed and another and he never came. I knew I couldn't ask Ma again, so every week I asked Aunt Vera, "You sure you gave my daddy the right address?"

Aunt Vera's real quiet, not like Daddy at all. She does her best to see me as much as she can since Ma don't want her 'round the house. When we moved here, I could tell Ma was itching for a fight with Aunt Vera. Think she was still mad 'bout having to leave behind her house and Vicksburg. She'd mumble about how she was tired of Uncle Clark looking down his nose at her till finally he told Ma and Aunt Vera there was "too many grown folks under his roof." I heard Aunt Vera crying that night, begging Uncle Clark to let us stay, but the next morning she started looking till she found us the house we stay at now. Ma looked through Uncle Clark like he was a ghost till the day she packed up our suitcases again, put them in the trunk of the car, and moved out.

Aunt Vera had folks from church drop off their old furniture to help get us settled, but Ma said, "Vera ain't got no kind of backbone." Looked like she had a back to me, but I can't ask questions when Ma starts her fussing. Most old folks start talking sweet in their older years, forgetting your name and calling you "Honey" and "Sugar," but Ma don't forget nothing, 'specially the hurts.

Every time Aunt Vera came by to take me shopping for clothes, or to drop off money for Ma, I asked her 'bout my daddy soon as I got in the car. She'd hold my hand and say, "We don't know when your daddy will be home Lymon, but, God willing, it will be soon." So, I waited some more. It was just me and Ma for so long, I almost forgot I had a daddy.

I got up from the curb and wiped the dirt off my pants. Walked down Third Street till I reached the diner. Only remembered then I was hungry. I had a few pennies in my pocket I took from Ma's purse. Not enough to get anything good. I stood watching through a big front window. That's when I felt a hand on my shoulder.

"You look like a cat outside a fish store," the man said. He was tall and thin as my daddy. Head full of white hair. He looked clean from head to toe.

"I'm heading in for breakfast, could use a little company," he said. "You hungry?" he asked me. My head said one thing, but my empty belly had a mind all its own. Said "yes" 'fore I could even think twice.

"My name's Eugene," he said, and stuck out his hand for me to shake.

"Lymon," I told him, and shook his hand hard like Grandpops taught me.

He opened the door and a bell banged against it as I walked in behind him. We sat in a booth with soft seats. Felt like sitting in the back of Aunt Vera's car. Everybody at the counter sat on stools attached to the floor. The black and white floor made me think of Grandpops playing checkers with his friends. After a little bit, the waitress walked over holding a pad and a big book she handed to Mr. Eugene.

"Morning, Eugene," she said smiling big.

"I'll need a menu for my friend, Lymon," he said while he was looking through the book. She smiled at me too, went back to the counter and brought me the menu Mr. Eugene asked for. I can count on one hand the number of times I been in a restaurant. Don't remember ordering from a menu, so I just watched Mr. Eugene reading, and then I looked down at the menu too.

Sometimes just looking at words makes my head hurt. Ma tells me I need to pay attention more. Teacher tells me to concentrate. But don't none of that work when the words all run together on the page.

When Mr. Eugene said, "Two eggs over easy, bacon, side of toast," I said, "I'll have that too."

"You barely looked at the menu," Mr. Eugene said. I pretended to look at it for a minute then say, "No, that's what I want."

The waitress took both our menus back. Mr. Eugene yelled behind her, "Tell Otis don't burn that toast like last time."

"So, Lymon," he said, leaning back in the booth. "No school today?"

"No sir," I told him.

"Holiday, is it?" he asked.

"Think so," I said, wondering how long it's gonna take for the food to come.

We sat quiet for a bit. Even though Mr. Eugene's hair was all white, you can tell he was a good-looking man when young. "A looker," my grandpops used to say. I asked him once if I was a looker. "You'll do just fine with ladies, Lymon, don't you worry," he told me. But I still don't know if that meant yes or no.

Mr. Eugene was wearing a white jacket over his clothes, so I asked him why.

"Keeps the hair off me," he said, smiling for the first time.

That's when I started wondering if this food was worth sitting with an old man who wasn't right in the head.

"The hair?" I asked. But then the food came, steaming hot and smelling so good, I needed to make my mouth stop from watering.

"Eugene's a barber," the waitress said to me. "His shop is down the street."

"You couldn't even let the boy guess," Mr. Eugene said to her, pretending to be mad.

I wouldn't have guessed that in a million years.

"Finish up, Lymon," he said to me. " 'Cause after you finish breakfast, you are gonna get that nappy head cut."

I was eating so fast, I barely heard him.

ELEVEN

Milwaukee, Wisconsin 1943

MR. Eugene's barbershop smelled a little bit like Ma's medicine, and I told him so.

"That's just the aftershave," he told me. "I use it to help keep your skin from getting razor bumps. Lot of the fellas think it smells pretty good."

"Really?" I asked.

"You said you live with your grandma?" he asked. "Vera Williams is her daughter, right?"

"Yessir, that's my aunt Vera."

"She's on the usher board at Calvary Baptist. I'm a deacon there," he said.

Looking at him again, he reminded me of the deacons back in Vicksburg who stood tall and straight in the front row during service and collected the money baskets from the ushers.

"She said she moved her family up here. From Vicksburg, right?" he asked.

"Yessir," I told him, wondering when he was going to stop talking and start cutting my hair.

"Good, fine people, Vera and Clark," he said. "Me and Clark sing in the Men's Choir every third Sunday. Speaking of Sundays…" he said slow, "when am I going to see you in service?"

I was too 'shamed to tell him me and Ma stopped going to church soon as Grandpops passed. Ma said she couldn't be bothered with "church folks, spending all their time on their knees. What did praying do for me?" I knew then she was talking 'bout Grandpops dying.

But I didn't say all that. I told him, "Soon as my ma gets better."

Mr. Eugene smiled and patted one of the chairs and told me to get on up.

"When was the last time you had this head cut?" he asked.

I shrugged my shoulders.

Sometimes Ma wrapped a towel 'round my shoulders and took out her scissors and cut it herself if she was up to it. Most times I didn't get it cut at all. Grandpops used to take me to his friend's house for a trim and he would give me a piece of hard candy to suck on while the two of them talked and talked, seemed like all afternoon. He spent more time talking than cutting.

Sometimes it hurt too much to comb my hair, so I'd just pat it down best I could.

Mr. Eugene took out a towel, then one of those big capes, and tied it 'round back.

"Mr. Eugene, I don't have no money for a haircut," I told him.

"Did I ask you about money for a haircut?" he said.

"No sir, but…"

He spun me 'round so I faced the mirror. I looked so small sitting in the chair, I made myself laugh.

"You see something funny?"

"No sir," I said, and put my head down.

Mr. Eugene turned on a shiny radio to a song I'd never heard before. My head started bobbing up and down.

"Now, how am I going to cut your head, with you boogie-woogieing out of the chair?" he asked, wiping down his scissors.

"Sorry," I said, trying to stay still. Aunt Vera bought Ma a radio when we moved to the house, but Ma only let me play it quiet, when she was resting in bed. Said it gave her a headache. I think the music reminded her too much of Grandpops.

When Mr. Eugene started cutting my hair, he talked about how long he owned this barbershop, about his wife passing, his daughter in Chicago. I put my head up then.

"Chicago?" I asked him.

"Yup. You got people there?"

"My momma lives in Chicago."

"Well, you can keep Chicago," he said. "Too big, too loud, too dirty for me," he said, laughing.

"So, you been?" I asked, staring at him in the mirror.

"Oh yeah. I visit about twice a year, but my daughter knows she got to come on back home to Milwaukee if she wants to see her old man any more than that."

"One day, I'm gonna go to Chicago. To visit my momma," I said.

"That so?" he said.

Mr. Eugene took a long time cutting, his scissors seemed like they never stopped moving. Started getting dizzy with him moving me this way and that in the barber chair. Ma just cuts real quick and we're done. But Mr. Eugene wasn't in no kind of rush. He asked me questions like I was the most interesting person in the world. About school, and my daddy. I didn't plan on it, but I told him all 'bout Grandpops. Sitting in that chair, with him cutting and the music playing, made me never want to leave.

Finally, he said, "Looks like we're all done here, Lymon." He took out a brown bottle and dabbed something smelled like medicine on my neck and 'round my forehead. He untied the cape and shook off all the hair. Then he brushed my neck with a little broom. Tickled so bad, I had to laugh. When he turned me 'round to the mirror, I barely recognized myself. Looked like a handsomer me. *A looker.* This haircut wasn't nothing like the ones Ma gave me. All 'round the edges was sharp. When Mr. Eugene held up a mirror in back, I could see even the hair 'round my neck was cut.

"Wooowee, that looks good," I couldn't stop myself from saying out loud. I looked like one of the boys from school who wore the nice shirts with ties every day. Probably who didn't sleep in the same room as his grandma and put salve on her swolled legs every day.

Mr. Eugene laughed.

"How much you charge for a cut like this?" I asked, still looking in the mirror and patting my hair like a girl.

"Told you already. This one's on me."

"But s'pose I wanna come back again?" I asked.

"I think we can work something out."

He lowered the chair and I shook his hand again, hard. "Thank you, Mr. Eugene. Nice meeting you."

"And nice meeting you, Lymon. Next time you have a holiday, you stop by and see me." He winked at me.

Mr. Eugene looked like he wasn't nobody's fool. I don't think he really believed I was on a holiday from school, but he didn't make me feel like my teachers at Fourth Street. Didn't laugh and call me a liar like they did. I wasn't 'bout to feel 'shamed 'bout leaving a place I never wanted to be in the first place. The less I went, the more I felt that way.

I walked out the barbershop feeling better than when I walked in. Wished we had a mirror at home so I could look at myself a little longer. I headed out again past the streetcars. Made my way down to Lake Park, where I sat and threw rocks for a while till school would let out. Then I headed on home, hoping Ma was in bed sleeping. I thought up a story to tell her about Mr. Eugene cutting my hair. Had a story all made up in my head to tell her. But by the time I reached the front porch I remembered, Ma probably wouldn't notice.

TWELVE

Milwaukee, Wisconsin 1945

I never wanted Ma to be sick, but the days when she had a hard time getting out of bed, was the days I didn't have to go to school. Ma didn't tell me I could stay home, but she didn't tell me I had to go either. Long as I fixed her some toast and a cup of coffee, put the salve on her legs, she didn't ask me 'bout nothing more. Ma stayed in bed longer and longer, and even though she was fussing more too, I could hear her voice sounded more scared than mad. Same reason she didn't let me sleep on the couch at night, I think was why she didn't want me going off to school on her bad days. She was 'fraid of being alone. On the days I stayed home, I'd turn on the radio soft and take out the guitar and play. My teacher told me once they would send someone over to my house if I missed any more days, but I never told Ma. Figured the teacher was trying to make me 'shamed like she did when she asked me to go to the board to do a problem or read a page out loud.

But one night just as we were sitting down to supper, we heard knocking.

"Go see who's at that door," Ma yelled. I nearly tripped over myself at first thinking Daddy was back so soon. Me and Ma never get company, so I knew it wasn't no visitor. Could see in Ma's eyes she was scared about the knocking. Me too. Never known Daddy to knock, but I kept hoping it was him all the way till I opened the door.

"Good evening, young man," a white man said. Tall with those blue eyes Ma says look like the devil and yellow hair. "Are your parents at home?"

I shook my head no, hoping Ma couldn't hear, and I could get him to leave.

"Is there another I adult I could speak with?"

"Who's that, Lymon?" she yelled from the kitchen.

"I don't know, Ma."

"Maybe you should come back another time," I said soft.

I hoped the man didn't hear her cursing as she got up from the chair and made her way faster than she moved in weeks to the door. She almost pushed me out the way when she saw who was standing there.

"Are you this young man's guardian?" he asked Ma.

"I'm his grandmother if that's what you mean." One thing 'bout Ma, you can't try any fancy talk 'round her. Don't nothing scare her.

"Well, I am Mr. Donnelley from the Milwaukee School District. We have a report of a young man, Lymon Caldwell, eleven years of age, who has been absent from Fourth Street

Elementary, let me see here...." He looked down at some papers on his clipboard.

"He's been sick," Ma said, not waiting for him to finish.

"Excuse me, ma'am?" the man said, looking past Ma to me.

"I said, he's been sick."

"I see. Is he sick now, ma'am?" he asked.

"He's better now. Ain't you, Lymon?" Ma asked. She didn't even turn to look at me.

"Yes ma'am."

"You are aware, ma'am, that he is required by the state of Wisconsin to attend school? Truancy is a violation of compulsory law and if he does not meet a basic attendance requirement then it is within our right to impose a fine or—"

"I said he's been sick."

"I understand that, ma'am, but he will either need to see a physician and provide documentation or—"

"He'll be in school tomorrow," Ma said, and shut the door.

My heart was beating fast. Partly 'cause I wanted to hear more of what that man had to say, and partly 'cause I wanted to see how mad Ma could get. I didn't have to wait long 'cause he knocked again.

Ma swung open the door.

"Ma'am. I wasn't finished. May I have your name please. For my records."

"Lenore Caldwell."

"And you said you are the boy's grandmother."

"Yes I did." I was behind her but I could tell she was rolling her eyes.

"And where are the boys parents?"

"You need to put that on your paper too?" she asked with her hand on her hip, looking down at his pad.

"Are you his legal guardian?"

"You see anyone else here?"

I could see the man's face getting red, and I was listening close so I could remember to tell Daddy every word.

"Ma'am...Mrs. Caldwell, I am sure you understand I have a job to do. And I need to ensure that every child in the district is receiving an adequate—"

"And...I...said...he'll...be...in...school...tomorrow," Ma said slow like she was talking to someone too dumb to understand. Her voice was getting loud now.

That man knew he got all he was gonna get out of Ma 'cause this time when she closed the door in his face, we didn't hear no more knocking.

Ma limped back into the kitchen. Her face was sweating now.

"Get me my medicine." I ran and got it.

THIRTEEN

Milwaukee, Wisconsin 1945

WHEN I woke up this morning, Ma was already out of bed, and I know that means today I gotta go to school. Our beds are so close they are almost touching. All night I gotta hear Ma snoring and wheezing, sometimes passing gas. When we first moved here, I wanted to sleep close to her. With Grandpops gone, everything 'bout being in Milwaukee was new and scary at the same time. But I can't ask Ma questions like I asked Grandpops. And he used to tell me stories and tuck the blanket right up under my neck at night, just the way I liked it. Ma don't do that.

"Get to bed" means time to turn out the lights and no more talking.

I asked once if I could sleep in the front room, on the couch. Felt like I was getting too big to be sleeping with my ma like a baby. She near bit my head off.

"S'pose I need something in the middle of night?" she yelled, coughing. "I gotta hope you hear me screaming for help?"

"No, Ma." I didn't ask again.

I got up this morning and pulled on my pants. I knew I

was getting taller when my pants started creeping up around my ankles. I put on dark socks so no one would notice, but I'd need to ask Aunt Vera to take me shopping. I know her and Uncle Clark ain't rich, but she always manages to find a little something to take me shopping when the weather turns cold or my pants can't be let out any more. Over at her church there's bags of clothes for people who need them, and if her money's too tight, she'll bring me something from the church bag. Ma says her clothes are just fine, but they ain't. Most of her dresses are worn and raggedy, and her winter coat is shiny 'round the elbows, but she don't go out much anymore so all she wears around the house is her nightgown and stained housecoat. I found a shirt that looked halfway clean and pulled that on. I washed my hands and face in the bathroom, brushed my teeth with the baking soda Ma makes me use. Ma was sitting at the kitchen table when I walked in, head in her hand.

"You okay, Ma?"

"What you think?" she said, sounding tired.

It's the same answer every time, but I keep asking. "You need anything 'fore I go to school?"

"Get my medicine from the bedside table."

I grabbed her bottle of coughing medicine and brought it back.

"What am I gonna do with this without a spoon?" she yelled.

"Sorry, Ma," I said, and grabbed a spoon from the sink and rinsed it off.

Ma poured two big spoonfuls into her mouth.

"Put my salve on before you leave," she said, and handed me the tin tub on the kitchen table. I opened it and tried to breathe through my mouth so I didn't have to smell the nasty smell of boiled eggs and mint. I dipped in my fingers and then spread it over the sores on Ma's legs.

"Ma, you got a new one." I pointed to another spot on her leg.

She sucked her teeth and didn't look. Her legs were big and dark and swolled. Last time doctor came, he said they had "fluid" and said she needed to stay off her feet. He said she needed to be in the hospital for treatments or she could lose her leg. Ma said doctors just try to take what little money she got. In Mississippi, Grandpops took her to the doctor every week. But in Milwaukee, she just don't go.

I wiped off the salve on my pants and headed to the door.

"Bye, Ma."

"Don't slam that—" I heard her say, just as I slammed the door extra hard and ran down the stairs. Only had to walk down two blocks to get to school, but I walked as slow as I could. I could already see the smoke from the factories past Cherry Street filling up the sky. I was almost at the school when I remembered I didn't have my books, but that don't matter much to me. School stopped mattering a long time ago.

I walked the two blocks down Third Street and made a left to Fourth Street Elementary.

In class I sit all the way in the back. Most everyone lives in the part of town I don't, where they got mommas and daddies working and living in nice little houses over near Eighth Street. Not that far away, but a whole lot different from Lloyd Street where I live. I know now school's going to be the same every year, but the teacher this year is the worst one I had in my four years since coming to Fourth Street. I hear Miss Desmond talking about the lesson, but I ain't listening much. Can hear the scratch of chalk on the board and the kids flipping through pages. I put my head on my desk and close my eyes. Ma's snoring kept me 'wake most of the night.

"Lymon? Lymon? This is a classroom, not a bedroom!" Miss Desmond is standing over me. I sit up quick and look around to see near everyone looking at me smiling. A couple of them laugh.

"Yes ma'am."

"You are barely here as it is. You'd think you could at least pay attention when you are in the classroom." Miss Desmond's a lot like Ma. She's talking but not really wanting you to say nothing back. A couple of the kids start laughing.

This class is like two classes in one. Up front are all the girls, in back are the boys. Miss Desmond's just as sweet as cherry pie when she's talking to the girls up front, but in the back, she spends all day yelling at boys, about their homework and fidgeting in their seats. But even then, she saves most of her mean for me.

"Do you think you can answer the problem I've written on the board?"

I look to front of the classroom and look around some more. Everyone waiting.

I don't need to look at the board to know I can't answer the problem.

"No ma'am," I say.

"I didn't think so," she says, happy with herself. She walks back up the row to Virginia Seals's desk up front. She's one of those girls who probably comes home after school and does all her schoolwork and drinks warm milk and eats cookies 'fore they go to bed. And her momma makes her hotcakes and sausage, and greases her hair then braids it up good and ties it with ribbons in the morning 'fore she leaves for school. Then her daddy kisses her on both cheeks and says, "Have a good day sweetheart." 'Course she knows the answer.

The teacher smiles big when Virginia shouts it out, and I put my head back down on my desk.

———•———

When I get home, I check on Ma. She's in the bed sleeping. The room smells like sweat and salve and cough medicine. I pick up the dirty bowl on her bedside table and put it in the sink. I grab Grandpops' guitar and head out to the porch in back. On the top step I sit and start plucking out a song Grandpops taught me 'fore he passed. He used to sit on my bed and show me where to put my fingers on each of the strings. His big hands on top of my little ones. At first my fingers couldn't reach all the strings, then when they could, he started me with real simple songs. He'd nod his head as I played.

"That's it. That's it. You got it," he'd tell me before we moved onto something new. Grandpops said I was "a natural" just like my daddy. But before I knew it, he started getting too tired to teach me more.

He'd say, "Not today, son. Your grandpops needs to rest a bit." Every day he was resting more and more till it seemed like he slept more than he was woke.

After Ma and the doctor said it was his heart, Aunt Shirley said it was more like a broken heart 'cause of Daddy being in Parchman. But I didn't know a broken heart could make you sleepy. More tired Grandpops got, more mad Ma got. Stopped going to church, stopped praying.

Today I played the last song he taught me, humming along 'cause I already forgot the words.

"What you doing out there?" I looked up, and Ma was at the screen door looking down at me. Ma don't never wait for no answer. "Get in here and help me get some supper going."

I walked back in the house and put the memory of Grandpops and his guitar right back in the corner.

FOURTEEN

Milwaukee, Wisconsin 1945

A few weeks after my first haircut, when my hair stopped looking as good as it looked that first day in his mirror, I walked by the barbershop on my way home from school, hoping I'd see Mr. Eugene. I stopped at the window and looked in. He was standing behind an old man, and there were men in seats waiting for their turn in his chair. When Mr. Eugene looked up, I waved from outside, and he came to the door.

"Back for another haircut?" Mr. Eugene asked. I was hoping he'd remember me, but I was still a little surprised he did.

"You think I need one?" I asked him. He made a big show of turning me 'round and looking on both sides.

"Looks like you could use a trim," he told me.

I showed him the money I had in my pocket. The money I took from Ma's purse.

"Put that away. I got a proposal for you." He pointed me to a seat.

I followed him inside. The radio was on loud playing the baseball game, but you could hardly hear with all the men talking. Sounded like the Cubs were losing bad against the Pirates with all the yelling and shouting curse words after every play. Others was talking about grown-men things. Mr. Eugene cleared his throat and said, "We have a young gentleman joining us." They quieted down some. Wasn't long though before they started up again.

I waited what seemed like an hour with Mr. Eugene and another barber cutting one head after another. He took his time with each one, just like he did me, each time taking out that brown bottle and putting some of the aftershave 'round the parts he just cut. Finally, Mr. Eugene came over and sat next to me.

"Lymon, I have a dilemma." Mr. Eugene told me his daughter went to college, but I think he must have gone too. I didn't know what half the words he said meant, but I found if I just kept listening, I could catch on. I kept listening.

"A dilemma?"

"I used to have a man who'd come around and help me out with keeping the shop clean. Sweeping up hair, wiping down the chairs, things like that, but I haven't seen him in weeks." I nodded. "Any chance you'd be interested in taking over a job like that? Say in exchange for some haircuts?"

"Yessir."

"Now I want you to think about it, son, talk to your grandma first."

"I don't need to talk to her. She won't mind." I didn't know if Ma would mind or not. But sweeping up some hair to get a haircut on the regular seemed like a good deal to me, and I wasn't going to let Ma stop me.

At school, a few of the older boys let me play football with them in the school yard on the days I came. I was the smallest of the group, but they let me stay 'cause I was the fastest too. Long as someone got me the ball, couldn't barely anyone of them catch me. If they did, they'd tackle me extra hard, but I kept right on playing. I was tired of the boys in my class, all too fancy, or too smart, or too something to be bothered with me. When the school bell rang after recess or after school, I said goodbye to the older boys, but not one of them invited me home to play. Called me "Little Lemon" and said I was still "a baby." Sometimes I came home from school with my lip busted up or with scratches on my face. When I told Ma I got them from playing, she told me, "You just watch to not tear up your clothes. Money don't grow on trees." I knew money didn't grow on trees, least not ours. But as far as I could see, it was Aunt Vera who had the job of worrying 'bout buying my new clothes, and she never once complained about not having a tree for money. Sometimes I wondered how Aunt Vera could be Ma's kin. Ma was loud; she was quiet. Ma was mean; Aunt Vera was nicer than nice. It was like Aunt Vera had to be four people all in one—an aunt, a grandma, a momma, and a daddy to me.

Mr. Eugene showed me where to find the broom and dust pan and the cleaning rags.

"Why don't you start over there?" Mr. Eugene pointed to the other barber's chair, where there was a pile of hair underneath, and I got to work. But first I took the rag and wiped the extra hair from the chair onto the floor, and then I started sweeping, real slow so I wouldn't miss any hair. I wanted to show Mr. Eugene I could work hard to earn my haircuts, maybe some extra money too. Before she got real sick, I'd watch Ma do the chores each week, scrubbing the house from top to bottom. Now between the two of us, we could barely get the dishes washed up after supper. Aunt Vera used to come and help straighten up, but when Ma told her she needed to mind her own house and not hers, she stopped coming around, and the house started getting messier and messier. Ma didn't notice or didn't care, I didn't know which.

———•———

Working for Mr. Eugene was the first job I ever had. Saturdays and sometimes Friday after school was the busiest day with men and mommas with their sons filling all the seats in the barbershop. I could barely sit down there was so much to do.

"Looks like someone just earned themselves a fresh haircut," he'd say after I finished. He'd take out a cape and I'd climb up into the barber chair. He'd turn to the music station channel on the radio, loud the way I liked it, and start cutting. In his chair, Mrs. Desmond, the lessons I didn't understand, and the boys who never invited me home, seemed 'bout a million miles away.

FIFTEEN

Milwaukee, Wisconsin 1945

I knew when I woke up something was wrong. Ma slept sound, snoring like a man. But this morning, her sleep sounded raggedy and she was sweating.

"Ma, you okay?" I asked her, shaking her a little.

She opened her eyes and looked at me but didn't say nothing. I got out of bed and stood over her. "Ma," I said again.

Ma looked like she didn't even know who I was.

"It's me, Lymon," I said close to her ear. I knew wasn't nothing wrong with her hearing, but I said it loud anyway.

Aunt Vera told me anything happen to Ma, I should go next door to Miss Dot's house, and she'll get word. So, I pulled on my clothes and ran fast as I could next door. Miss Dot had the radio in the kitchen up real loud and she didn't hear my knocking at first, so I ran around to the back door that goes into the kitchen. She was at the stove, and I near scared Miss Dot to death when I started knocking, but she turned down the radio and opened the door quick.

"What is it, son?"

"My ma…my grandma…next door…" I said out of breath. "Something's wrong. She's breathing funny and sweating too. Could you tell my aunt Vera?"

"I'll get my Lenny to get over there right away," she said. "Where's your grandma now?" she asked.

"Still in bed," I told her.

She walked back with me in her housecoat and slippers. She stood over Ma.

"Lenore. Lenore." She tried shaking Ma a little bit. "It's Dot from next door." Ma looked at Miss Dot same way she looked at me. Like she didn't know her. We been neighbors since we moved to the house, but Ma ain't never said more than a few words to her. Said she don't like folks too much "in her business."

"Go on and get me some water. Lemme see if I can get her to drink," Miss Dot said to me.

I ran into the kitchen and filled up a glass. Time I got back to the room, Miss Dot had Ma sitting up. I sat on the edge of the bed watching her give Ma water.

"Is Ma going to die?" I finally asked.

"Hush, Lymon," Miss Dot said. "'Course not. She needs to get to the doctor is all."

Ma was as quiet as could be, and Miss Dot stayed right there by her, holding her hand, praying soft. I was glad she was there 'cause seeing my ma in bed staring at nothing made me think about Grandpops and dying and being alone and all the things that made me most scared.

I heard the front door slam, and Aunt Vera came rushing in. We all helped get Ma in her robe and out to the truck.

"We'll drop you at the house, Lymon, and you stay there with Uncle Clark while I stay with Ma," Aunt Vera said.

"I can come with you," I told her. "Ma would want me to."

She thought on that. "All right then," she said, rubbing her hand over my cheek, and we drove fast as we could to the hospital, Aunt Vera praying all the way.

———◆———

It was after midnight when we got back to Aunt Vera's. The doctors at the County Hospital told us to go on home. Said Ma should have been brought in a long time ago. Said she was "in serious condition." Didn't know when she'd be able to go home. Said she might even lose her leg. I felt sick to my stomach then. Ma couldn't hardly get around on two legs, let alone one.

Aunt Vera made up a lumpy couch in her front room with blankets and a pillow. As much as I wanted to sleep alone on the couch at my house and not in a room with my ma, I was missing her now, almost wishing I could hear her voice fussing at me once more.

Momma

ONE

Milwaukee, Wisconsin 1945

Every day we waited for news from the doctors, and every day they told Aunt Vera they were waiting on Ma to get "stable." When I asked Aunt Vera what that meant, she told me to "just have faith."

Aunt Vera and Uncle Clark worked long hours at Falk Foundry over on 30th Street. Between me and Ma, Cousin Dee and her babies, their money had to stretch every which way. Some days they'd work so long, I'd only hear Uncle Clark's snores to know he was home. I had to walk farther to school from Aunt Vera's house, but she and Uncle Clark made sure I was there every day. Even my teacher noticed after I was at school two weeks straight.

"Are you *finally* taking school seriously?" Miss Desmond said one day in class.

Aunt Vera tells me hating on folks is the Devil's work, but she ain't never met Miss Desmond.

Aunt Vera may have worked a lot, but her house was clean, and she always kept food in the icebox. She looked like a little bird, afraid of her shadow, but she worked like she was two times her size and never once complained. She did her share of praying though. For Ma, for my daddy, for her daughter Dee and her grandbabies, for her son I barely remember who fought in the war and never came back. Figured her knees must be sore from all the time she spent on them.

When I went to church with her on Sunday, Aunt Vera prayed some more with Uncle Clark right 'long beside her whispering, "Yes, Lord. Yes, Lord." Up in the front row, I could see the back of Mr. Eugene standing taller than the other deacons. Aunt Vera jumped out of her seat every time the choir sang, clapping loud and singing along, so I had to stand too.

The singing sounded the same as it did in Vicksburg, but here, I saw they had an organ for the hymns and a piano for the choir. The organ player was up front, pounding the keys and rocking from side to side, almost drowning out our singing. Back home at church, all we had was a small piano Grandpops said was always out of tune. I looked down at my hands, moving my fingers pretending to play along with the organ. *Piano fingers*, Grandpops called them.

After church, downstairs at coffee hour while Aunt Vera and Uncle Clark were talking to Reverend Lawson, and I was eating up half the pound cake, Mr. Eugene came up behind me and said in my ear, "Don't forget to leave some for the deacons." I nearly spit my cake out laughing. "I won't," I told him. He winked and said, "I'll see you on Saturday."

Soon as Mr. Eugene gave me the cleaning job at the barber

shop, I told Aunt Vera all 'bout it. She said she was proud I was a hard worker, just like my grandpops. I noticed she didn't say my daddy. When I told Ma, she had asked, "How much is he paying?" When I told her I was getting free haircuts, she had grunted and said, "You get free haircuts at home." I nodded, but the next Saturday, after I fixed her breakfast and gave her her medicine, when I told her I was going to the barbershop, she didn't say nothing more.

Just when I was starting to get used to living back with Aunt Vera, everything changed.

One night, 'round midnight, I heard whispers at the front door and then smelled a room full of perfume.

"Daisy, it's late," Aunt Vera said, sounding mad. I was so tired, I wasn't sure if I was dreaming.

"You said to come, so I came," I heard a voice say. Felt like I heard the voice a long time ago, and then there she was leaning over me on the couch in the dark saying, "Lymon baby, c'mon and get up. It's your momma."

"Let me get his things together," Aunt Vera said. She turned on the lamp in the corner of the room. Felt my feet moved to the floor and someone sit down at the end of the couch.

Uncle Clark came in, tying up his robe. "It's the middle of the night. The boy's still sleeping."

"Lymon, sweetie. You remember me?" She smooshed her lips all over my forehead.

I didn't say nothing. But when I looked at the woman sitting at the end of the couch, it was like I was looking at myself. Never thought I looked anything like my daddy. We're both skinny and have those long fingers Grandpops always talked about, but apart from that, see us out in the street, not sure you could place us as family. But looking at my momma was like looking in a mirror. Same eyes, small and squinty, same big, shiny forehead. Only on her, she wears it proud, with her long hair brushed back into a ponytail, like she's showing it off. Same small nose, smashed flat at the end, just like mine.

"Well, well," she said looking right at me. We sat like that for a minute until Aunt Vera said, "Daisy, I have some things for him in my room."

"Well, hurry up, Vera, I gotta long drive back to Chicago."

"Why didn't you just come in the morning?" she asked.

My momma turned her head quick. "Some of us have to work in the morning, Vera. I had to borrow my girlfriend's car to get here. 'Sides, I couldn't wait another minute to see my baby. Was you all kept him from me all these years. Now he needs his momma." She smooshed her lips on my head again.

"Daisy, please stop…"

Uncle Clark stepped closer to my momma. "Ain't a need for all that, Daisy."

But my momma kept right on talking.

"No, you stop, Vera. If your momma hadn't gotten sick, she would've never let me see my child."

"I don't have time for this. Lymon, come with me." Aunt

Vera took my hand and pulled me up. "You've got to gimme a minute to get some things together for him," she said, and walked me into the kitchen.

"Aunt Vera. That's my momma?" Still didn't know if I was dreaming.

"Yes, Lymon, that's her." Aunt Vera was whispering now. "I'm sorry, honey. I didn't know what else to do. With Ma sick and all, me and Clark are going to have to take some double shifts to pay her medical bills. We just can't care for you right now. I had to get in touch with your momma, and she's real excited about you staying with her in Chicago. Now, soon as we know what's going on with Ma, and your daddy comes back through, you may be able to come on back, but for now…" She didn't even finish. She took her sleeve and wiped her eyes.

I could hear my momma and Uncle Clark, still loud talking in the front room.

"What's gonna happen to Ma?" I asked.

"We putting it in God's hands, Lymon. She'll probably be at the hospital for a bit. Maybe stay here if I can get my shift changed. But I need you to just hang on with your momma, okay? She's got a steady job there, and I hear her husband is a good man."

"You gonna tell Daddy where I'm at?" I asked her.

"Soon as I see him, Lymon, yes, I will," she said.

"And then he's gonna come and get me?" I asked.

"God willing."

Think that's Aunt Vera's way of saying she don't know much more than I do.

Been wanting to see my momma for so long and now here we were in the same house, and this feeling wasn't nothing like I thought it would be.

Just like that, I'm going to Chicago and going to live with my momma, all in one night.

TWO

Chicago, Illinois 1945

I been two places my whole life, Vicksburg and Milwaukee. Three if you count Parchman prison. Now, I can add in Chicago. Mr. Eugene told me his daughter lives somewhere in Chicago, and she comes to visit every now and then. Said this city is too big for him. But the minute I saw all the buildings, the lights and cars, I knew it wasn't going to be too big for me.

My momma talked as fast as she drove, like she's making up for all the years we been apart. She told me 'bout my little brothers, "bad and badder" she called them. Talked so fast I almost missed their real names, "Orvis, after his daddy, 'cause Lord knows I wouldn't've of picked that name" and "Theo, after *my* daddy." She stopped long enough for me to ask her, "You pick my name too?"

"Lord no!" she shouted. Seemed every other word she said she shouted.

"Thought your grandmama told you every dang thang. Think that was your daddy's grandaddy or some mess like that. I don't remember." She kept right on talking.

In between Momma talking about what a good man her husband Robert was and how bad Theo and Orvis were, she talked a little 'bout meeting my daddy back in Vicksburg. When my daddy told the story, was a lot of parts about how pretty my momma was and what a good dancer. When my momma told it, Daddy couldn't do nothing quite right.

"That fool had two left feet," she said, "but I danced with him anyhow. Ooooh, Grady could play a harp though, I'll give him that. And he was a smooth talker. If I wasn't so young and stupid, I wouldn't have listened to half his mess," she said, shaking her head.

"Him and his people was always walking 'round Vicksburg like they know what don't stink. But we knew better. And your daddy with his high and mighty self sitting up in Parchman." She sucked her teeth and laughed. "Wish I could have seen your grandmama's face then." She barely took a breath. "They never thought I'd make nothing of myself, but I did just fine. Moved up to Chicago with my sister when I was big with Orvis. His daddy wasn't nothing but a bag of promises either, but I finally found myself a *good* man." Said the word *good* like Robert was Jesus Christ himself.

"Now, Robert ain't what you call *easy on the eyes,* but I found out a long time ago, being easy on the eyes don't pay the bills." I didn't know if my momma was talking to me or herself. "Some folks down at my job got a lot to say about Robert being on the older side, but what man wants an old woman?" Momma hit me with her elbow. "Lymon, you awake?" I was tired and wanted to close my eyes, but I was 'fraid I'd miss something important. So, I kept listening. I listened less though when she started on 'bout my daddy. She seemed like she had a lot to say 'bout someone she didn't want nothing to do with. But I kept quiet 'bout that. She didn't ask nothing 'bout me. 'Bout school or Ma. Even 'bout Grandpops. Finally, I asked. "You know my grandpops died?"

"Oh yeah, I think I heard that." But then she kept right on talking again.

I never got to know her momma and daddy. But Ma told me once they were drinkers. "The worst kind," she said. "Po-lice at their house all the time. Those people don't have no dignity. Don't even have a church home." Last few years, Ma didn't have one either, even though Aunt Vera's church, Calvary Baptist, was right down the street. Think Ma felt like God gave up on her. Aunt Vera must have talked to Reverend Lawson 'bout her family 'cause it was Calvary Baptist helped us out with furniture, and bringing by baskets of food 'round the holidays. She told me once, "If those church folks want to give, then I'm gonna receive." She put on a little fake smile when they dropped off the basket. We ate up all the food and Ma didn't say nothing more about it.

———— · ————

It was too dark to see much on our drive, and Momma drove so fast, some of the road signs were blurry.

"You like music?" I must have drifted off, 'cause my momma was shaking my arm.

"Yeah, I like music. Daddy and my grandpops taught me—"

" 'Cause they got a good radio station out here." She turned on the radio and started snapping her fingers to a song I never heard before. She couldn't carry no kind of tune. "Your daddy told you I was the best dancer in Warren County?" The car started to move from side to side a little bit when she started shaking her shoulders to the music.

That was when I remembered I left Grandpops' guitar back at Ma's house.

"Momma!"

She kept singing.

"Momma!"

"What, Lymon? You hear me singing?"

"I forgot my guitar," I told her.

"Your what?"

I turned the music all the way down.

"The guitar Grandpops gave me. I left it at Ma's...at my grandma's house."

"Well, we can't do nothing 'bout that now," she said.

"But—"

"I'll get a better guitar than some old beat-up one from your grandaddy." She laughed. "Chicago has plenty of guitars."

But I wanted Grandpops' guitar. The one he taught me my very first song on. When I played that guitar, I could hear his voice and feel his fingers on top of mine. I closed my eyes again trying to go back to sleep, but even if I wanted to, my momma's singing kept me awake.

THREE

Chicago, Illinois 1945

WE turned onto a wide street with big, pretty trees on the sidewalk, and she slowed down. All I could hear was the car engine as I was staring up at the street sign, trying to read the name when my momma said, "This street here is one of the nicest on the South Side. We're gonna move here once Robert gets his raise," she said, smiling.

Looked like a street where rich people lived. Every building had big windows with fancy curtains pulled back so you could see the lights on inside.

"Colored folks live here?" I asked her. She stopped smiling like I just woke her up from a sound sleep. " 'Course colored folks live here. Didn't I just tell you we gonna move here?"

"Is Robert rich?" I asked her.

"Not yet, but he's gonna do just fine. You'll see. He's not like most of these sorry men, happy with some change in their pocket. Robert got dreams." I didn't say Robert would need a lot more than dreams to live on this street. He'd need a tree for money.

She started driving fast again, telling me 'bout the furniture she'd seen in a store downtown she was going to have to buy to fill up their new apartment. Just when she was talking 'bout silk curtains, we stopped on a street called St. Lawrence and started looking for a place to park.

"Our place is right there." She pointed to a brick building across the street.

This street looked nothing like the street my momma wanted to live on. Even though it was late, people were walking around and sitting on steps like it was daytime. Instead of trees on the sidewalk, one building had garbage piled up in front. Seemed people in Chicago never went to bed. Chicago made Milwaukee look like Vicksburg. Wondered if there was another city made Chicago look as small as Milwaukee.

"'Fore we go on up to the apartment, there's a few things we need to get straight." When my momma talked slow, I could hear more of the Vicksburg in her voice.

"My man…my husband"—she showed me the band on her finger—"he don't stand for much foolishness. I told him I had to come and get you, and he was real good about it, seeing you ain't his folk and all. You or Orvis, but he loves me. You just do like he say, and he'll be good to you. You understand me, Lymon?"

"Yes ma'am," I said.

"And I don't want none of that 'yes ma'am' stuff, you hear me? We ain't in Mississippi. 'Sides, I'm your momma, ain't I, not your ma'am." She leaned across the seat and pinched my cheek so hard it hurt. Kissed me wet on my forehead. She put lipstick on while she was looking in the mirror and parking the car at the same time. I took my bag and we walked to an apartment building in between a long row of a lot of other apartment buildings.

"This the one?"

"Yeah, this is it!" she said, loud again. "What were you expecting? The Drake Hotel?"

The hallway was dark, but I could follow her just by the smell of her perfume. Ma never wore any, said it was the sign of a "low" woman. But my momma smelled real nice.

"We're up on the second floor," she said to me in the dark. Then she said softer, "This place is just for now."

I barely had time to even ask what job Robert was getting his raise from before we were at the door.

━━━◆━━━

Robert was a big man. Looked 'bout as wide as he was tall. Had a thick mustache and hair Mr. Eugene would need 'bout an hour to get through. He looked old enough to be my momma's daddy. He was sitting on the couch when my momma opened the door, and he wasn't in any hurry to get up.

"Robert, here he is. My baby. My Lymon. Lymon, go say hello to Robert." She pushed me to the couch.

"Hello, Mr. Robert," I said, holding out my hand trying not to stare at the belly sitting on his lap.

He looked at my momma and laughed. "He ain't but a little

thing," he said. "My Theo's almost as big as you, and he's only seven."

"He's petite like his momma, right, Lymon?" Momma pushed me forward some more.

Wasn't sure I liked the word *petite*.

"Nice to meet you, Mr. Robert," I said again, my hand still out.

He grunted loud and stood up. Clapped me on my shoulder and I dropped my hand. "Good to meet you, Lymon." He hiked up his pants. Said to my momma, "Took y'all so long?"

"Don't get me started. Vera wanted to give me a hard time 'bout waking up my boy in the middle of the night. Like she's his momma." She laughed.

"I'm going to bed," Robert said, stretching. His shirt rose up good then, and I saw most of his hairy belly up close. Don't know how my momma could look at that every day, but she didn't seem to notice. Just kept right on smiling.

"Make yourself at home." He laughed again, pointing to the couch.

"I'll be right in, Robert," my momma said. Sounded like every time she said his name, she was singing a song.

"You gonna have to sleep on the couch, baby. Just till we move into our new place. The boys are already tight as it is.... You understand, right?"

I nodded.

She went and got a blanket and pillow from her room. She

kissed me on my forehead and handed them to me. "You and Robert are gonna get on just fine," she told me. "He's been good to me and if you treat him right, he'll take care of all of us." I didn't know what my momma was talking 'bout, but I nodded my head.

" 'Night, Lymon," she said. "Try and get some sleep."

I tucked the sheet into the cushions tight where Robert's big behind made them flat, laid the blanket on top. I could hear Momma and Robert in the room laughing 'bout something. I hoped it wasn't me.

Even though my momma turned off the lamp, the room was still bright from the street lamps outside the window. I took off my clothes and folded them up. When I lay on the couch, all I could feel were the springs. But the pillow smelled like lilac perfume. Just like my momma.

FOUR

Chicago, Illinois 1945

I woke up expecting to see my momma. 'Stead I saw four big eyes staring down at me.

"You Lymon?" the older one asked.

"You Orvis?" I answered.

"I'm Theo," the little one said.

These were my momma's boys. *Bad and badder.*

"Leave that boy be and get to the table!" I heard Robert yelling from the other room. They were sitting down eating 'fore I could even sit up.

"You sleep all day back in Milwaukee?" Robert asked me.

"No sir. What time is it?" I asked, pulling on my pants.

"I look like a clock to you?"

Bad and badder laughed.

"Don't I gotta go to school today?" I asked him.

"That's on your momma. But she's working first shift today. She'll be home 'bout four." Momma told me she works on the line at the Campbell's factory over on 35th and Western.

"All day long, pressing tops for those dang soup cans," she

said, when she talked about her job. When I asked her if Campbell's gave out free soup to people who worked there, she looked at me sideways. "Now how they gonna make money if they giving away free soup? I work on a factory line, not on a soup line." She nearly cracked herself up laughing.

Robert grunted and sat on the chair to tie his shoe, huffing and puffing the whole time. Thought he was gonna bust every button on his shirt his belly was so big.

"Don't you leave this house while we're gone, you hear me?"

"Yessir."

"Now I know you and your folks only been up North a short while, but I am a born-and-bred *Northern Negro*. That means I don't want to hear all those 'yessirs' in my house. You're not in a cotton field, you in Chicago, boy. Act like it. You got to call me something, call me Mr. Robert."

"Okay," I answered. Not sure what to say now.

"Okay what?"

"Okay, Mr. Robert."

"Orvis, Theo, get your behinds out here," he yelled. They ran to the door, and the three of them left slamming it behind them. I went to the table to see what was left of breakfast and looked like between the three of them they ate up most of the eggs and toast. I ate what was left off one of the plates and started looking 'round.

Wasn't much to see of the apartment but I took my time. Theo and Orvis shared one small room off the kitchen, barely big enough to fit a bed and dresser. Made me think of me and Ma sharing a room back in Milwaukee. Wondered if she was out of the hospital yet. Wondered if I'd hear from Aunt Vera and how long it'd be before she could tell my daddy where I was. I wanted Daddy to show up and put Robert in his place. Maybe Momma see Daddy again, she'd leave old Robert in the dust? But then what about bad and badder? Just needed to see my daddy to talk to him about all that was going on. I looked in Momma and Robert's room too. Their room was bigger, and it had one big bed with a side table and a lamp. A chair with Robert's uniform jacket and pants with suspenders still on them. Underneath his sweat, I could smell Momma's perfume. On the dresser, she had perfume bottles and lipsticks lined up in a row on a fancy white scarf. Up above it was a mirror. I opened the top drawer and saw all her ladies' things, some real fancy in shiny colors with lace. Felt 'shamed to be looking, so I closed that dresser so fast one of the perfume bottles tipped over.

Back in the front room was the flattened-out couch, two lamps, and a kitchen table and chairs. Wasn't no place for me to turn 'round good, but I could tell by looking out the front window all the action was outside. Even though it was early in the morning, out on the sidewalks were people talking, selling, laughing. And I was stuck up here. Wasn't nothing left to do but go back to sleep, so I sat back down and waited.

———•———

I heard loud voices then a key in the door. Orvis and Theo ran into the room.

"Lymon! You still here?" they asked me.

"Where else would I be?"

My momma had on her work clothes, a dingy blue dress and lace-up shoes with thick bottoms. She set down her purse on the table.

"You still in bed?"

"No. Well, I fell asleep, I guess. Robert... Mr. Robert said I couldn't go outside.... You gonna put me in school?"

She was looking through some mail. "Yeah," she said. Still flipping. "I gotta change my shift to get you up to the school, Lymon. I just started this job. You want me to get fired?"

"No. But, can't Mr. Robert take me?"

I ain't never one day wanted to go to school, but if it meant I could get outside and see what was happening in Chicago, I was ready to go.

"I'll ask him."

"Tomorrow?"

She rolled her eyes. "Least you could have done was washed up these dishes." She started slamming the breakfast dishes into the sink.

"Yeah, why you didn't wash the dishes, Lymon?" Theo asked.

"I'm going to lie down. Lymon, take these two outside for a bit. I got a headache." Momma went into her room and closed the door behind her.

Theo and Orvis tore out the door and down the stairs. When we reached the stoop, they said, "Take us to the candy store."

Just like in Milwaukee, Chicago got lots of stores. But here they got a funeral parlor next to a hair salon next to a church next to a pool hall. Don't make much sense to me. Everybody's in a hurry, so I walked faster, catching up to Theo and Orvis. We turned onto 43rd Street. The street numbers never went this high in Milwaukee. I saw some men in real fancy suits, in colors and one with thin stripes. I was thinking I'd look real fine with a suit like that. Man smiled at me when he saw me looking hard at his suit.

"Stop staring," Theo said, pulling my hand. Every woman was prettier than the next, hair done up nice, but none as pretty as my momma. She always had on some kind of makeup, but you could tell she'd be just as pretty without it. Wonder what happened between Milwaukee and Chicago make people look so good. A whole city full of lookers. I was wishing now I had a fresh haircut from Mr. Eugene. Maybe Momma would get me some new clothes too. I heard a loud sound above us and Orvis told me that was the el train. I wished Aunt Vera could see that in Chicago trains run on tracks as high as the buildings instead of through town.

We kept walking till we got to the candy store. Theo snatched up about half the store with his greedy self, and I had to put some back in the bins.

"How much money you got?" I asked him.

He pulled out a pocketful of change. All the money I took from Ma's purse here and there never added up to that much.

"You take that from Momma's purse?" I asked him.

"My daddy gave me this," he told me.

"Daddy always gives us money for candy," Orvis told me. *Daddy?*

"Why you call him Daddy if he ain't your daddy?" I asked Orvis.

"He's just like a daddy. 'Sides, I ain't never met my real daddy, but Momma says I ain't missing much."

"Where's your daddy?" Theo asked.

"He's travelling now with a band. But he's coming to get me soon."

"To take you back to your people?" Orvis asked.

"Not sure where we're gonna go, but we're gonna be together real soon." Sounded just like Daddy then.

"You don't like Chicago?" Theo asked. He was big and fat like Robert, but his face was round and sweet as a baby's. Skin was as soft and smooth as one's too.

"Chicago's all right, but I need to be with my own daddy." I put some candy pieces back in his hand, grabbed a few for myself and hoped he didn't ask me why I didn't want to be with my momma.

From the minute she picked me up in Milwaukee, I knew that what Ma told me all along was right. You can't make someone into a momma that don't want to be. And I didn't want to lie to that sweet face.

FIVE

Chicago, Illinois 1945

MOMMA finally got 'round to signing me up for school at Lincoln Elementary. And just in time too. Thought I was 'bout to go crazy sitting in that apartment everyday waiting for her to get home from work. Started looking forward to taking Theo and Orvis outside, bad as they was.

Robert worked downtown in one of those high-rise buildings as an elevator operator.

"I never been in an elevator," I told my momma.

"Well, you don't want the job Robert has, baby. All day long white folks talking to you like you got no sense. It ain't all bad, but it's gonna be better once he gets in the union."

I don't know anything 'bout a union, and I ain't said nothing 'bout wanting to work an elevator, just wanting to ride one, but it seems like my momma only listens to half of what I say.

"That's gonna mean some real money," she said. "And then we're gonna move to the place I showed you. And I can finally leave Campbell's and stop smelling like soup every dang day."

She smiled so big and wide, like she really believed it. I wondered if my momma waited on my daddy's dreams too.

Momma had to go in late the day I started school, and she talked about it all the way there.

"They gonna dock my pay," she told me like it was my fault. She was walking so fast I could barely keep up. Didn't ask her why Robert couldn't take me, since he took the boys to school every morning.

Lincoln Elementary was white brick instead of red like Fourth Street and at least two stories higher. Seemed like every building in Chicago was tall. In Milwaukee we had grass in the yard where we had recess and that's where I played football. Wouldn't be no playing football here with the whole school yard concrete. There was a swing set, but that was for babies, not sixth-graders.

Kids in this school look more like me than the ones in Milwaukee. Half of the boys needing haircuts, no one wore a tie, and their shoes were as run-over as mine. Think all the kids from fancy families went to school in another part of town, maybe over where Momma wanted to live.

———————

In the school yard, out at recess, right away I could tell there was one boy who was gonna be trouble. Big ole fat boy like Robert. Acted like he owned the school.

He came over to me quick. "Where you from, little man?" He put his sausage fingers on my shoulder.

"Milwaukee," I told him.

He squeezed my shoulder so hard I thought I heard bones crack. "Welcome to Chicago, Milwaukee." He smiled, a big gap in his front teeth. Another boy came running past, and he shoved that boy so hard he fell down flat on his face. Nobody said nothing. The boy got up, wiping his face and kept moving, like he tripped himself. Big boy strutted away like he was President Truman himself.

Two boys near me said, "You the new one, right?"

"Yup," I told them.

"You best not mess with Curtis," one told me.

"Who, fat boy?" They laughed then. "He don't scare me."

"Well, you better keep that to yourself," the other one said. Looked like Curtis scared them pretty good.

"I'm Errol," the taller one said.

Little one said, "I'm Clem."

"Lymon," I told them.

"You said you was from Milwaukee? I been there once to visit my cousins," Clem told me. He told me names, but I didn't know any of his folks. He talked so much I forgot we just met.

At lunch I sat with them, eating our dry ham sandwiches. Recess I stayed with them in the school yard. Clem was small and fidgety, jumping all over the place and never stopped talking. But Errol was real quiet, like he got a lot on his mind. I fit right in the middle.

With Clem and Errol, I didn't mind going to school as much as I used to. Schoolwork was still the same, lunches just as bad. So were the teachers, but it got me out of the house and out of Robert's face.

I stayed out of fat boy's way. Thought he forgot all about me too, till one day I felt his hot breath on my neck behind me in the school yard. Could see on Clem and Errol's face it was him, but I just kept right on talking.

"Le-mon," he sang in my ear.

I turned to see his big smile. All around everyone was getting closer trying to see what was going to happen next. He stepped close to my face, but I didn't move. My forehead reached right about to his chin. He must have missed a grade or two. Ain't no way he was only eleven.

"C'mon, Lymon," Errol said, pulling me away.

But I could see if I ran now, I'd always be running.

"You heard your friends? Go on, Le-mon," he said.

"I ain't in no hurry," I told him. He looked surprised for about a second, then shoved me in my chest with both hands. Felt like I was hit by a truck. I'd been shoved by the older boys at my school, and hit by the back of Ma's hand. Wasn't no way I was going let this boy do it too. I walked back to him, and he shoved me again.

"Hit him, Curtis!" I heard someone yell.

"Hurry, teacher's coming," a boy whispered.

When I turned around, I saw Errol and Clem looking scared for me, like they knew I was going to get beat bad. I could see Mr. Harold walking over toward the crowd of us, and I balled my fist hard and swung with everything I had. Curtis was so busy looking for the teacher, he didn't see my fist coming. Knocked him dead in his nose, and the blood went flying. Some squirted on my shirt but most dripped on his. He looked down at his shirt, then looked at me. Looked at me then his shirt. Pretty sure I heard Errol laughing behind me.

"He got him," Clem said, like he was proud.

The teacher snatched up both of us and Curtis still hadn't said one thing to me. Everybody in that school yard was staring at me. In my old school, they looked at me like I was nothing. "Lemon," living with his old, raggedy grandma. But here in Chicago, nobody knew that Lymon, and I aimed to keep it that way. Grandpops once told me a man has got to demand respect. After seeing Curtis's face and everybody else's, 'specially Errol and Clem, I think I did just that.

SIX

Chicago, Illinois 1945

AT home, there wasn't no getting away from Robert. Didn't take me long to know we wasn't going to get along. He always looked like a bomb ready to go off whenever I was in the room. Guess he was waiting for an excuse, and wasn't two weeks in 'fore he found it.

That elevator job must have been as hard as Momma said 'cause Robert came home some nights looking mad as can be. Those days I just stayed out of his way. Went down to the stoop or walked 'round back and watched boys play stickball. I knew football and tag, but never learned how to play any of those games with a ball and bat 'cause I was in the house so much with Ma, but I liked watching. Daddy said, soon as he was home long enough he'd show me.

Every night Robert got home and every morning he woke up, he looked like he just remembered all over again I was sleeping on his couch and eating his food. Even though was me now had to take the boys to school, you'd think he'd ease up on me some, but he wanted to know what took me so long in the bathroom, why I folded my blanket the way I did, and did I ever close my mouth when I ate my food? Momma didn't say one word, like she didn't hear nothing he said. Sometimes when he wasn't home from work, I'd ask Momma if she heard anything yet from Aunt Vera 'bout my grandma, but she'd just shrug.

"No, Lymon. I told you, your people only get in touch with me when they need something."

"But she didn't send you a letter or nothing?" 'Course she'd roll her eyes at me then.

I couldn't believe Daddy hadn't been in touch yet. Made me wonder if it was me he didn't want to see or Momma.

My ma wasn't the best cook, but my momma can't seem to make nothing taste good. Don't no one seem to notice but me. Her fried pork chops are dry and the beans barely got any seasoning. I was pushing food 'round on my plate, thinking about Ma.

"Food ain't good enough for you?" Robert asked me.

I looked down at my plate still almost full of food. "I ain't that hungry."

"You think I work all these doubles to feed this family for you to throw away good food?" he asked me.

I looked at Momma, but she was wiping Theo's mouth.

"What you looking at your momma for when I'm talking to you?"

"No sir."

"No what?"

"No, Mr. Robert," I told him.

"We don't waste food in this house."

I started eating, hoping I didn't choke to death on those dry pork chops.

Next time Robert started in, he didn't waste his time talking. It was late when Robert got in from work. Most times we were all asleep, but there were some nights when no matter how hard I tried, I couldn't stop thinking 'bout my daddy and sat up at the window. I heard his key at the door and tried to get to the couch quick, but not before he saw me. I pulled the covers up and closed my eyes.

"What you still doing up?" he asked.

Just like I used to do with Ma, I pretended not to hear him. I closed my eyes tighter.

I heard him breathe heavy, take off his coat, and then I relaxed.

But when I opened my eyes, Robert was looking right down at me.

"Get up," he said soft.

"I'm sleeping," I told him.

With one hand, he snatched me up so fast, I felt like I was flying. Used his other hand to take off his belt.

"What did I do?" I asked him.

"When I ask you a question, you answer me. You gonna pretend like you sleeping, when I just saw you up. You think I'm stupid, boy?"

He didn't wait for me to answer. His belt hit my side. Hit it again two times quick. I wondered how many times Robert thought was gonna be enough for pretending to be asleep when my momma came out.

"Robert?" she said.

Not Lymon?

She looked so young standing behind him. Like she must have looked when my daddy first saw her at that dance years before.

"Momma, I—" He hit me again.

She never even told him stop. Looked at me like it was me making him do it. I didn't yell out like he wanted me to. If I had, he probably would've stopped sooner. Each time the belt hit my backside, I thought about how I could hurt him back worse. Not now, but when he wasn't expecting it. Maybe I'd wait till he was sleeping good. I could take a whipping. Been taking Ma's whippings for years, but he was putting all he had behind it. My knees was getting loose and I bit down on my tongue and swallowed the blood.

"Okay, Robert," my momma finally said, touching his arm real soft, like she wasn't sure.

"Step out of line again, and you got more of that coming, you hear me, boy!" Now I could hear Theo crying in the room.

"Hush up in there," he yelled.

"Maybe your daddy's family ain't taught you nothing, but I sure will," he said.

What you gonna teach me my daddy's family ain't? Was all I could do not to say the words in my head back to Robert. He could see on my face I was thinking something.

"You got something you wanna say to me, boy?"

"No sir," I answered, knowing he wanted me to call him *Mr. Robert.*

"Didn't think so. *Now* you can go to sleep."

Finally, he put his belt back 'round his big ole waist.

My momma asked Robert if he was gonna eat the plate she left out for him.

"Lost my appetite," he told her, and went down the hall to the bathroom.

I don't think Robert ever lost his appetite. When Momma walked past the couch, I turned over so she couldn't see my face. I waited all this time to be family again with my momma. Come to find out, I wasted a lot of time wishing for something I didn't even know if I wanted anymore.

Lying down on the couch that night with the springs poking in my side, the hard part in me went soft. I ain't been to church in I don't know how long, but I prayed like Aunt Vera and said to God, whispering again and again, "Please God. Please tell my daddy to come and get me."

———•———

Never thought being at school would be better than being at home, but it was. After our fight in the school yard, I didn't have no more trouble from Curtis for the rest of the year. Errol and

Clem stuck to me like I was their bodyguard. Three of us would laugh the way Curtis would find someplace else to be whenever I came to lunch or recess. 'Side from Errol and Clem, most everyone else stayed away too. But the three of us got along just fine. One thing I liked 'bout the two of them, they didn't ask a whole lot of questions. Maybe they were scared I'd do to them what I did to Curtis, or some of the other kids who made me mad, but on the days when I came to school, so sore I sat with my leg tucked up under me or with a busted lip or my eye swolled, they didn't ask one thing. And that was just the way I wanted it.

Having Errol and Clem as friends was a lot like having Little Leonard and Fuller. Sometimes I wondered if they ever thought about me. Or I tried to picture what they looked like now. Or what it'd be like if I'd stayed in Vicksburg. Errol and Clem made listening to teachers and getting through the day a whole lot easier. Think Errol didn't much like school either, but Clem was a different story. I could tell he understood everything the teacher was talking about. I saw him slip his homework papers on the teacher's desk when he got in in the morning. During spelling tests, he was the first one finished, but he covered his paper when the teacher handed back the grades. "A" is what I saw marked on his paper when I got 'bout three words right. One day when he opened his satchel, I saw it was filled with books. I think Errol knew about Clem too, but it was the first time I had someone to sit with at lunch. I wasn't 'bout to ask him why he spends so much time on his schoolwork.

With Theo and Orvis gone most of the summer staying with Robert's sister in Indiana, it felt like back in Milwaukee when I spent all day by myself. I missed taking them to the candy store and the park, but most of all, I missed Errol and Clem.

I saw Clem out on the street one day with his two pretty sisters, but they didn't let him stop and talk. Clem yelled from across the street, "Lymon, call the police. They're kidnapping me!"

The younger one knocked him on his head, but I could tell she was laughing. Made me miss Theo and Orvis a little bit then. When I asked my momma why I couldn't go with them to Indiana, she told me, "Frannie got kids of her own, Lymon. She's doing us a favor taking my two. And I can't ask her to take three." So, I spent just 'bout the whole summer walking the streets of Chicago like I walked the streets of Milwaukee, doing my best to stay out of Robert's way.

When school started up again, and nearly everyone was going into seventh grade at Haines Junior High, I heard Curtis was going to some other school all the way cross town.

SEVEN

Chicago, Illinois 1946

THE weather was just getting cold enough we didn't even want to be outside at recess. Me, Clem, and Errol stood close to the door, rubbing our hands together, hoping we could go in soon. Wasn't much I missed or even remembered 'bout Vicksburg, but I did miss the warm, sunny days most the year. And never having to worry 'bout wearing warm clothes.

"Someone's calling you," Clem said, pointing to the fence near the sidewalk.

"What are you talking about?" Clem spends most of his time joking so I never know when he's playing games.

"Over there." He pointed again. "That man over there just called your name."

I turned and looked. And there, on the other side of the school-yard fence, was my daddy.

I took off running.

I was out of breath by the time I reached him. I touched his fingers through the chain. My daddy looked like he just walked from Milwaukee to Chicago.

"Daddy! Where you been?" I just about screamed through the fence.

"Been looking for you." He smiled big like always. He pointed down to the fence opening and we walked down to where we could see each other face-to-face without the fence between. I hugged him tight not caring who saw me.

Felt like I never wanted to let him go. My head was now just about at his nose.

"You trying to outgrow me, boy?" My daddy laughed.

"Is Ma okay?"

"Ma is Ma," he said. "Gonna take a lot more than some sugar disease to knock her out. She was in the hospital for a while, and she's staying with Vera and Clark now." He looked at me serious. "They had to take her leg, Lymon, part of it at least. But she's still getting around."

"She ask about me?"

"All the doggone time! You know she ain't none too pleased you up here with your momma, but there just wasn't no other way. Couldn't put no more on Vera and Clark right now."

"You come to get me?"

"How'd I know you were gonna ask that? How's it here living in Chicago with your momma?"

"You know she's married, right?" I told him.

"Yeah, I heard that."

"Well, he don't want me here. I don't think Momma does either."

Daddy was still smiling, but I could see his forehead crinkling in the middle like it does when he's worrying.

"Me and Robert ain't getting along."

"Your momma know?"

"Yep. But she's always on his side."

He thought on that for a bit. I heard the bell ring.

"Daddy, I got to get back to school. You gonna be here when I get out?"

"No, I just stopped by to say hello and bring you this." First time I noticed he was holding a case. A guitar case.

"You brought my guitar?" I hugged him again.

He handed it to me. "Didn't want you forgetting all the songs your grandpops taught you." He smiled big again.

"Lymon, c'mon," I heard Errol yell.

"Daddy, when am I gonna see you again?" Feel like I been asking this question my whole life and never getting the answer I want. But I keep asking hoping for the answer I want to hear.

"I'll be back real soon, Lymon. I can promise you that. Just taking care of some loose ends, and I'll be back for you."

"For good?"

"For good. You hang on, you hear me?"

I tried hard not to let Daddy see how hard it was to say goodbye, not knowing when I'd see him again. Didn't know if I could hang on till the wind changed again. Maybe the guitar could take some of the hurt away, but every day with Robert felt like when Daddy talked 'bout doing his hard time at Parchman.

"I will," I told him. And I almost believed it.

I caught up to Errol and Clem, the guitar case banging against my leg.

"That's your daddy?" Clem asked.

I could see Daddy making his way down the street, looking old and tired.

"Yup. He brought me my guitar. Really my grandpops', but I got it after he passed. My daddy's a musician." Don't know why I couldn't stop the words from coming about Grandpops and Daddy. "He just dropped this off till he comes back to get me."

"Never knew you played guitar," Errol said soft, like he didn't know who I was anymore.

Clem pretended he was an emcee, making his voice deep and loud, "Presenting our entertainment for the evening: the one, the only, Lymon Caldwell. What will you be performing tonight young man?" he said, holding out his pretend microphone to me.

"Get away from me, Clem," I said, smacking down his hand. The three of us laughed then and went on inside.

I know Clem was playing outside when he held up the microphone, but all day long, I kept seeing myself up on stage, hearing Clem's words: *The one, the only, Lymon Caldwell.*

EIGHT

Chicago, Illinois 1946

I thought having Grandpops' guitar would make things better, but it just made everything worse. After my daddy came, I thanked God for hearing me. But he must have forgot all about me again.

First thing, Momma wasn't none too pleased when I came home toting a big ole guitar case.

"What do you think you're bringing in my house?" she asked.

"Daddy brought it! He brought my guitar," I started to take it out and show her.

"Uh-uh." She put out her hand to stop me. "We don't have no room in here for that. 'Sides, what's Robert going to say?"

The case Daddy bought me was real pretty. Black with red velvet inside. Two big buckles and one handle to carry it.

I stopped short. "Robert?"

"Your daddy happen to give you any money while he was handing out guitars? Does he know that feeding you ain't free?" I wondered how much my momma gave my ma and grandpops to feed me all these years, but 'course I didn't ask that.

I shook my head no.

"I didn't think so. But he wants to give out guitars.... Put it over there in the corner and let me talk to Robert when he gets home."

"You wanna hear me play?" I asked.

"I got a headache, Lymon."

First time since I been there I think she saw something in me wasn't right, 'cause then she said, "Maybe later. You want to play, go on down to the stoop."

———————

When Robert got home from his double shift that night, I was just about asleep. Heard him in the kitchen smacking on the plate of food Momma left out on the stove for him. When he went in the bedroom, I heard her whispering soft, and heard her say "guitar." Heard Robert's voice louder, but my momma started talking sweet, and his voice got quiet again. Soon I heard him snoring.

———————

At breakfast, Robert came in and sat down, sleep still in his eyes.

"Heard we got our very own Muddy Waters in the house?" Robert said to me.

Theo asked, "Who's Muddy Waters?"

"A guitar-playing negro, just like our Lymon here."

"You play guitar, Lymon?" Theo asked.

"Yup, my grandpops and daddy taught me." Wasn't no way Robert was going to make me feel 'shamed 'bout that.

"Wish I had time to hear one of them tunes, but some of us got to work. Your daddy know anything 'bout working or just strumming guitars?" He laughed. "'Cause it's my working putting food in his son's belly."

"My momma's working too," I said, taking the last bite of my eggs.

His hand hit the side of my head so hard, I felt dizzy.

"What'd you say?" he screamed.

I looked him dead in his eyes. I stood up holding the spot on my face he hit. He stood over me. "Ain't my momma working to feed me too?" I asked.

"Did I ask you about your momma working? Your daddy so high and mighty he gotta leave you here under my roof? You just make sure I don't hear none of that guitar playing when I'm around, you hear me?"

I nodded.

"Now get your Muddy Waters behind to school!" Me, Orvis, and Theo scraped our plates and made our way to the door.

The streets were so loud with the el train above us and the music from the pool hall at the end of the block, but the three of us walked to school quiet that morning. I got to my seat just as the bell rang. Errol whispered something from the seat behind me.

"What'd you say?" I asked, and turned around.

"Your lip is bleeding," he said.

I wiped it off with the corner of my shirt and laid my head on the desk.

NINE

Chicago, Illinois 1946

FIRST thing I do when I get home, is take out my guitar. Got to make sure Robert's working a double and make sure Momma ain't taking a nap. But if it's just me, Theo, and Orvis, I can play all I want. They sit right up under me, watching my fingers on the strings. I show them, just like Grandpops showed me. I let Orvis try a bit, not Theo though. Ain't no telling what he'd do. Momma is right 'bout bad and badder, but they love listening to me play. One day when I played "Sweet Home Chicago," Theo snatched up Momma's hairbrush to use as a microphone, and started singing, *"C'mon, baby, don't you want to go..."*

I thought I'd pee my pants laughing. Orvis danced in back of him, stepping side to side, and we pretended we were a group.

"Well, well..." Momma said from the doorway.

We were laughing so loud, we didn't hear her come in. But she was laughing too. "Look at my band of boys."

We played music until supper, and without Robert, I could eat and talk in peace, just the way I liked. After supper, Momma gave me a bill from her purse and told me to run to the corner store to get some pops, while Theo and Orvis did their school-work. She never asked much 'bout mine. If she did, I told her I did it at school. She was lying down by the time I got back, so I put the pops in the icebox and washed up and got ready for bed.

Any day is a good day I don't have to see much of Robert, so when I pulled the blanket up under my neck, I didn't even mind the springs tonight. Robert got in late and didn't say two words to me, just went straight into bed, dead tired. Between the moon and streetlights, the room was lit up like the Fourth of July, shining in my eyes. I got up to close the curtains and nearly fell over my guitar case lying in front of the window. Momma told me, I don't keep it in the corner, Robert's likely to throw it with the trash, so that's just where its been at.

When I went to stand it back up in the corner, I saw one of the buckles was undone. Something told me to look inside. My guitar was lying there, just the same as always, looking better than ever in that pretty red velvet. When I went to pluck one of the strings though, I saw one was loose. Just hanging there. *Robert?* The house was quiet, and I could hear the start of his heavy breathing. I was so mad, I wanted to shake him awake. I took a couple of steps to their room and stopped. *Theo and Orvis.* I walked fast across the room and opened their door. They were awake and looked like they were waiting for me. Orvis looked at Theo and I could see he was already crying.

"Theo did it!" Orvis said, pointing. "When you went to the store—"

"You don't touch my guitar, you hear me!" I said in his face.

"I just wanted to see if I could play it!" He was crying loud now.

"Ssshhh, shhh…" Me and Orvis tried to keep him quiet.

"But you busted a string and now I—"

I went to the bed and put my hand over his mouth. Snot was running down his face onto my hand. I never seen babies cry as big as Theo cried.

"Hush up, Theo," Orvis said in his ear.

I felt a hand around the back of my neck.

"Who you think you talking to?" Robert said real low into my ear. "You putting your hands on my boy?"

Theo and Orvis sat scared, looking from me to Robert. And finally, Theo stopped crying.

"This is my house. And that means, anything in here belongs to me and mine. You pay rent here?" He turned me around to face him.

I felt my fists getting tight.

"You deaf?"

"No," I said.

"Didn't think so."

"I broke his guitar," Theo cried again loud.

"Go on to sleep!" Robert yelled and pulled me out of the room, closing their door behind him.

In the front room, he stood in front of me. "Seems like this guitar is causing more problems than it's worth. That what's happening?"

"No," I answered.

"See, that ain't what it seems like to me. 'Cause I'm up in the middle of the night talking about some foolishness when I should be sleeping. So I'ma tell you what. I have any more problems with you and this damn guitar, it's gone. You got that, Muddy?"

He didn't wait for my answer 'fore he turned and went back to bed.

Even though Robert was working doubles, I didn't touch my guitar for seemed like weeks after that. Even when Orvis begged me to play a song or Theo promised he would never touch the guitar again, I still said no. But sitting at my desk in school, or lying on the couch at night, I'd play the strings in my head, seeing Grandpops' hand over mine or hearing Daddy playing right along with me. I could see me and Daddy, maybe Ma too, in a little place in Chicago.

"This is my daddy." I'd introduce him to Errol and Clem. I could just hear Daddy making them laugh.

At night, I could play my guitar all I wanted.

One night when Robert's snoring sounded like the el train coming through the apartment, I got up, opened the case and took out my guitar. Grandpops kept the guitar polished with a little white rag. He told me once he saved 'bout a year to buy that guitar 'cause there wasn't nothing he loved more than music. Said first time he heard a record on his uncle's phonograph, he thought he'd died and gone to heaven. He scraped and scratched till he finally ordered it from a catalog, and after he taught himself to play decent, realized he liked playing for himself 'bout as much as he liked playing for a crowd. Ma said he paid more attention to that guitar than he did to her.

"Spent half the day polishing it," she said. But I don't think she was mad, 'cause when Grandpops was playing music, he'd make everybody happy. Daddy's the same. "We three are all music men," Grandpops told me.

His voice wasn't much, but it was good enough to carry a tune. He said my daddy took to music right away, knew I would too. He said as a baby I'd smile big just listening to him play. "This one here is gonna be playing the Cotton Club one day, you'll see," he told my ma.

"Hope not," she said back. "An honest day's work is what he needs to be doing, not running around to every little juke joint, trying to hustle up coins," she told my grandpops.

"Now you know the Cotton Club ain't hardly no little juke joint, Lenore. And me and you gonna be sitting right in the front row, looking clean as can be." He kissed Ma's neck and made her laugh. He was 'bout the only one who could.

I sat back on the couch and let my fingers strum over a few strings real soft. It didn't sound the same with one string missing. I stopped and listened to make sure Robert was still snoring. He was. I strummed again. I tried to remember the last song

Grandpops taught me, but I couldn't get my fingers to line up quite right. Finally, the song came back slow at first and then picked up. Made me smile just thinking how Grandpops loved to hear me play. And then the door to my momma's bedroom opened.

Robert was on me 'fore I could even move. He snatched up the guitar and threw it against the wall so hard I could hear the wood crack and break into pieces. I jumped up to get it and he stepped in front of me.

"Sit down! When I tell you I want quiet, you listen. And that means I don't wanna hear no country-ass guitar strumming in my house in the middle of the night when I'm trying to sleep!"

My fists was balled so tight, I wondered if I could just hit him hard, as hard as I hit Curtis, and knock him out cold.

Momma came rushing out the room, tying up her silk robe. "What's going on?"

"He broke my guitar," I answered, even though she was asking Robert and not me.

She looked where I was pointing. Then looked at Robert.

"I can't sleep with all his guitar playing. Now you want me to get some sleep after working all day or you want me to listen to this boy playing all night long?"

"Lymon, I told you you got to play that outside."

"It's late," I said to her. I knew nothing I said was going to make any difference. Already she was standing close to Robert, trying to make sure he wasn't mad at her.

"Go on to bed Robert, I'll take care of this."

This?

Robert turned and went back to bed. I went to the guitar, holding the strings going every which way in my hands.

"Why you always making it so hard on yourself?" Momma asked pulling her robe tighter. Her lipstick was smudged, and she had dark circles under her eyes.

"I couldn't sleep," I told her. But all at once, I felt so tired, I didn't feel like I could keep my eyes open.

"Well, I told you, and you didn't want to listen."

Kneeling on the floor, in front of Grandpops' broken guitar, I looked at her then. Stared her right in the eyes that looked just like mine. Wondered what she saw when she looked at me. "You ever gonna take my side?"

"I ain't got time for this. I told you to play that thing outside," she said whispering.

"Robert's always right? You let him hit on me, break my guitar, and you ain't never gonna say nothing? I ain't got my daddy or my ma. I'm here in Chicago, and I ain't even got you?"

She took a deep breath. "I don't know who you think you talking to. I'm here ain't I? Your daddy ain't."

I walked over to the couch and lay down, covered up with my blanket.

"You think it's easy letting someone take your baby from you? Telling you, you ain't good enough? I'm doing the best I can to make sure you all getting what you need. Robert's trying to be a daddy to you."

I closed my eyes.

"Clean this up in the morning," she said.

She may have said more, but I wouldn't know. I fell sound asleep.

TEN

Chicago, Illinois 1946

FIRST thing I saw when I woke up was the broken guitar. And even though I slept sound, I felt tired all over again. Robert left early, Momma too. So, Orvis and Theo ate some toast while I swept up the pieces of the guitar and put them in the trash. Put the part that was still in one piece back in the guitar case, closed it up, and put it back in the corner. They tried hard not to look at me. Finally, Theo asked, "Want some toast?"

"Nope. Let's go," I told them. "We gonna be late."

Errol and Clem knew something was up. In class, I could hear Mrs. Robins talking and scratching out words on a board, but all I could see was my guitar, broken in pieces. I looked up when I heard one of boys in class I call country boy answer a question. Been here months and he's still wearing old overalls like he's a farmer down South.

His slow-talking, slow-walking ways don't belong nowhere near Chicago. Most everyone can take some horsing 'round at school. Everyone except country boy. After he went and told his daddy I been bothering him after school, he made me madder than Curtis ever did. Watched his daddy come to school, worried about his boy, and walk right in Principal Davis' office. Next thing, I'm sitting in the office listening to talk about "consequences." Had to stay home from school for a whole week. First two days, I left same as always, but then one day when I snuck back to the apartment, Robert caught me home, hit me good then told my momma she was "raising a juvenile delinquent." He was so mad you'd have thought it was his boy was suspended. Even when I could go back to school, I didn't. Spent days after I dropped off Orvis and Theo walking the streets of Chicago, thinking 'bout my daddy and wishing I had someone, anyone, to fight for me.

Since I got back to Haines, I been watching that country boy at recess and lunch, when he thinks no one's looking. He keeps a satchel full of books. Back at Fourth Street Elementary, teachers there would read storybooks, sometimes at the end of the day. It was about the only time I liked to hear their voice, acting out the parts. Reminded me of the stories Grandpops told me at night. I could close my eyes and pretend to be lost in there. But when the book closed, it was back to a class where I didn't belong. Every time I picked up one of those books to read on my own, I couldn't hear a story, just the stumbling of my own words.

I watched him one day, cutting through a fence 'round back that led over to Michigan. Told Errol and Clem, we oughtta follow him and find out where he's heading. But Clem said to leave him alone.

"Don't we got better things to do?" Clem said.

"Why you worried 'bout country boy now?" I asked, staring him down.

"Didn't say I was worried," Clem said smiling. Clem is always smiling. "I said, don't we got *better* things to do?"

Today, I ain't got better things to do.

At recess, I watched country boy walk over to the corner of the school yard, looking 'round to make sure no one saw him. I waited till he opened up his satchel and took out one of his books.

"C'mon," I said, tapping Errol and Clem, and walked on over, them behind me.

He wasn't expecting company. I stood over him and snatched the book from his hand. I made out the words *Weary Blues* by Langston something. I know Langston's country boy's real name, but I ain't used it since he got to Haines. Don't intend to neither.

Was him and his big mouth got me suspended from school. He still ain't paid enough for all that time I had to hear Robert's mouth every day. Beating on me every time he got in the mood. My momma telling me she "don't have time" for a boy who don't know how to act right in school.

"What's so interesting in this here book?" I asked him and opened to a page, pretending I was interested.

I read the words from the book out loud slow: "Yet...thou... hast...a...loveliness..." country boy was even crazier than I thought, sitting in a corner at recess reading a book like this. Like everybody else at Haines, he knows to keep his mouth closed when my mouth is open, but he must have been feeling bold. Laughed right in my face.

"You can't barely read," he said, looking up at me.

Know I heard Errol or Clem, maybe both of them, laughing behind me. All at one time, I could see this country boy and his daddy walking into school, looking like his shadow, and see my daddy leaving me behind again and again. And I could feel Robert's belt on me and my momma behind him, just looking on, and my broken guitar and the words from the book all jumbled up....

"If I can't read, country boy, you can't neither." I told him then. Wishing he was Robert and Momma and Daddy and the stupid teachers. And I tore one page after another from his book, just to see his face. He stood up tall. Looked almost as big as Robert then standing over me. I looked up at him. But what I saw when I looked at him was someone not scared but good and mad and tired too.

Tired just like me of taking a beating every day for something he didn't deserve.

"Pick up my book," he said low, just like Robert does when he's real mad. He grabbed my arm and twisted it so hard my knees bent. Errol tried to step in, but country boy wasn't having none of that. We stood like that for a while, eye-to-eye, ain't neither one of us want to give. I spit right in his face, but he didn't let go. Never heard a school yard so quiet.

When Mrs. Robins took us to the principal's office, I saw country boy smiling.

———•———

"Yet thou hast a loveliness…" If I had to read a book, I wouldn't waste my time on that mess.

ELEVEN

Chicago, Illinois 1946

WHAT changed most 'bout being at school after the fight with country boy, was I didn't have nothing to do with him. Momma said I get in trouble one more time at school, I'm looking at being sent away. Don't know where, but I know it ain't back to Milwaukee and Ma. Sure ain't with my daddy.

Me and country boy acted like we ain't never met. Didn't even look at each other. Wasn't like I was scared. Felt more like Joe Louis in the 12th round, like I'd lost some of the fight in me, but I was still standing.

The other thing was Clem. After the fight, seemed like he didn't want nothing more to do with me and Errol.

"What's wrong with him?" I asked.

"Don't know," Errol said as Clem stayed inside during recess again. We saw him once after school with country boy walking down Michigan. Looked like they were long-lost buddies. Don't know where they were going but I knew I couldn't ask. Me and Errol kept right on together, but without Clem, and Daddy, and without my guitar, seemed like I was walking in my sleep.

After Robert broke my guitar to pieces, I stopped going home straight after school. I walked the streets of Chicago till my feet hurt and got home in time for dinner. But one day, when it was too cold outside for walking, I came home early. Momma came in the front room after changing out of her work clothes and sat next to me on the couch.

"I'ma see about getting you a new guitar," she said.

"That's all right," I told her. Wasn't nothing gonna replace the one Grandpops gave. "I don't even feel like playing anymore."

"You just saying that now, but once I get you one of those fancy new ones, you'll go right back to playing. Robert's just been so tired these days. They giving him a hard time down at his job, promising one thing, and doing something else, but you'll see, he's a good man."

I couldn't even look at her. I was afraid she'd see on my face what was in my head. See all the hate I had inside for him and all the times I wished him hurt or worse.

All I could get out was, "Mmm-hmmm."

"Well, I'ma go lie down. Take Theo and Orvis out for a bit okay? And bring the mail up for me," she asked, pinching my cheek.

Soon as she said their names, they came out the room, ready to go. My head hurt something bad and today, all of the Chicago noises were just making it worse. Time we got back to the apartment, felt like my head was about to split in two. On our way up the stairs, I remembered the mail.

"Go on up, I gotta get the mail," I told Theo and Orvis, and ran back downstairs to get it. Right on top was a letter with a name I knew. *Vera Thurman*. I rushed up the stairs so fast, I nearly passed Theo and Orvis as I ran into the apartment, hoping Momma would read what Aunt Vera wrote. But there was Robert sitting his fat behind on the couch.

"Boys," he said, looking up when we came in.

"Hey, Daddy," Theo and Orvis said. I nodded my head.

"You got the mail there?" he asked me, holding out his hand.

"Something in here for my momma," I told him. Should have just shut up, but I needed to know what Aunt Vera wrote. When he didn't say nothing, I said, "Should I bring it to her?"

"Nah, just give it over here," he said, waiting.

I handed him the whole stack and stood there while he looked through. He turned to me.

"You ain't got nothing better to do than to watch me open mail?"

I went in the room with Theo and Orvis and watched them play jacks on the floor.

Daddy told me to hang on. And I promised I would. But I been hanging on longer than anyone should have to, and it was time I figured some things out for myself instead waiting for God and Daddy.

When I heard Momma in the kitchen, I came out, holding my head.

"What did the letter from Aunt Vera say?" I asked her.

"What letter?"

"One that came today. I gave it to Robert."

She shrugged her shoulders. "I didn't see any letter. I'll look later. What's wrong with your head?" she asked.

"Hurts. Theo and Orvis are too loud."

She stopped and held her head to the side, looking at me.

"Go on and lie on my bed while I'm getting supper started," she said.

"Where's Robert?"

"He had to go to one of his Mason meetings. He'll be home later. Go on ahead," she told me.

My momma's room looked out onto the street, but she kept a big curtain at the window to keep it dark. My momma's side of the bed had some clothes piled up from the laundry she was folding, so I had to sleep on Robert's side. I took my momma's pillow, so I could smell her perfume smell. On Robert's table, I saw the stack of letters I gave him earlier. Didn't think twice, I grabbed the stack and looked for Aunt Vera's letter. It was all the way at the bottom, opened. Her letter didn't have but a few lines:

> *Dear Daisy,*
> *I should have sent this sooner but we've been busy taking care of my mother. Please use this to help with Lymon. I'll send more when I can.*
>
> > *Send him our love,*
> > *Vera and Clark*

The sound from the el train made the room shake and my head pound harder. *Where's the money she sent?* I turned that envelope upside down, but wasn't nothing in there. Looked over on Ma's dresser and on her side table. Robert's work pants were hanging on the chair. I went over and dug my hands deep in one of his pockets. There at the bottom was four bills folded in half. I took them and put those bills in my front pocket. Laid back down on my momma's pillow. Another train went by and with Aunt Vera's money in my pocket, I knew then what I had to do.

Lymon

ONE

Chicago, Illinois 1946

I didn't need to wait long for Robert's freight-train snoring to start up before I pulled on my clothes, tied up my shoes, and closed the front door behind me.

I didn't mind walking. I could walk all the way to Milwaukee if I had to, but I was hoping instead to buy a ticket on a midnight special back to Milwaukee. Everybody in Chicago knows where to find the train station, so when I stepped outside, I asked the first person I saw, and they told me how to get there. When I got lost, I asked again.

Felt bad 'bout not saying goodbye to Theo and Orvis. And Errol too. Much as I'd miss Chicago, I'd miss them more. I wondered if Clem would even notice I was gone. Soon as I got back, I was gonna see Mr. Eugene about work, not for haircuts this time, but real money to help Aunt Vera and Uncle Clark. I think Ma'd be happy to have me back, have someone else to fuss at.

I kept checking to make sure the money was still in my pocket. That money was as much mine as it was theirs. Robert sure didn't do nothing to earn it. Had to be enough to get me to Milwaukee.

Never been out in the streets of Chicago this late at night. During the day Chicago looked like it was all about business, with everybody off to work and in shops, but at night, it felt like a party. Buildings were lit up and flashing with music pounding out of doorways. 'Long the way, I looked in every nightclub, hoping I'd maybe see my daddy. The men at the door would push me outta the way.

"Grown folks only, boy," they'd say.

But at one of the clubs, a man in one of those fancy suits standing at the door letting people in, let me stand just inside enough to see the stage and see the men up there playing. The club was small and so thick with smoke I started coughing, but I could still see someone tapping on a piano up on stage and some of those shiny horns that sound so pretty. There was a woman up there too in a sparkly dress singing. Her hair was done up all nice, and she was singing in the microphone like she was singing to her man. My heart was just 'bout beating out of my chest. If I didn't need to get on to Milwaukee, I would have stayed half the night. I remembered Grandpops saying when he heard his first record, he felt like he died and gone to heaven. Watching that band, I was right up there with them on stage and in heaven too. I could see how my daddy couldn't leave this alone. How the music pulled him from one town to the next. I played the strings of my guitar on my pants leg. Played right along with my eyes closed.

———•———

If I was going to make the train, I needed to keep walking, so I did, felt like all night till I made it to Union Station.

Looked like a lot of folks were looking for a midnight train 'cause even though it was late, Union Station was lit up bright. People were coming and going every which way. The names of places, spelling out MINNEAPOLIS, SIOUX FALLS, and OMAHA, places I never heard of, were all up on one big board.

I found a seat on a hard, wood bench next to an old lady. Looked like she had 'bout one hundred suitcases. I waited awhile to catch my breath. My feet felt like they were on fire.

"Excuse me ma'am," I said. "Can you tell me how I get to Milwaukee?"

"Well, you go right on over there"—she pointed at a sign said TICKETS—"and buy yourself a ticket."

"Thank you, ma'am."

"Think you missed the last train," she told me. "Next one ain't till tomorrow morning."

I didn't care how long I had to wait. I walked over and waited in line. When I got to the man at the ticket window, I said, "I need a ticket to Milwaukee."

He never looked up. "One way or round trip?" he asked, sorting through his papers.

I didn't answer. Finally, he stopped sorting and looked at me.

"You coming back to Chicago or not boy?"

"No sir," I said. "I'm not coming back."

He looked at me funny then. "Where's your parents?" he asked.

"I'm going to visit my grandma. She's sick."

"Can't sell a ticket to a minor. You'll need to bring your parents if—"

I turned and walked back to the benches. Needed time to think about how to get the ticket. Figured maybe I could ask the old lady to get it for me, but when I went back to the bench, she was gone. Suitcases and all.

While I was sitting and looking, thinking about who I could ask, I heard someone behind me ask, "You looking for someone, son?"

When I turned around, I saw blue uniforms and two police officers.

TWO

Chicago, Illinois 1946

THE sun was just coming up as they put me in the back of the police car. Momma and Robert were probably just getting up, on their way down the hall to the bathroom to get ready for work. As we drove, I looked out the window at all the streets and shops I walked past trying to make it to the train. All that just to end up right back where I started. Wondered where I was gonna go since Momma said they was gonna send me off if I messed up again. Robert probably had all my clothes packed up and sitting by the door already.

"Here we are," said the police officer who was driving. "Home sweet home." We parked in front of a white brick building, and they came around and opened the back door to take me out, up the stairs, and inside.

"Sit over there," they told me, and pointed to a bench.

The police station was almost as busy at Union Station. Police brought in people still fighting, took people out with their hands in handcuffs behind their back. Made me almost miss being back at the apartment. As bad as it was, I didn't want to miss a thing. The station felt like a pot 'bout to boil over.

"Excuse me, sir," I said as the police officer who brought me in passed by. I'd been sitting there for so long my behind was sore.

He stopped and stared down at me.

"How long do I have to sit here?" I asked him.

"Till we tell you that you can move," he told me.

"Is someone gonna tell my momma I'm here?"

"We did, and we're just waiting for her to arrive. Gotta feeling she's not gonna be pleased to see you here."

"Can I go home when she gets here?" I asked, trying to pretend I didn't hear the comment 'bout my momma.

"First you gotta see the judge. Officer Peterson will explain it all to you," he told me, and then walked away quick.

The judge?

I sat back and closed my eyes. I should have been sleepy what with being up all night, but I turned in the bench so I could see the door good, and waited for my momma.

"Lymon Caldwell," a police officer called out.

"Yessir."

"Come with me please," he told me. I stood up, not sure if my legs were shaking 'cause I was scared or 'cause I'd been sitting so long. I made them move along behind him, past the front desk, and out of the room with all the other folks that were brought in.

He took me to a quieter room to sit and wait on another bench. After a while, a police officer walked in with my momma behind him. She had on her work clothes, and it was the first time I seen her without her lipstick on.

"You just have a few minutes. He'll be going in to see the judge shortly," he told her.

I stood up when the police officer left the room.

"What the hell you doing here?" my momma almost spit at me. "After all we done, you gonna steal from us?"

"That was my money, from Aunt Vera," I said, mad too.

"And where'd you think you were going? To find your daddy?"

"I was going back to Milwaukee. To Aunt Vera and Ma, so I don't gotta have no one hitting on me all day long."

"I told you, if you just act right and give Robert a chan—"

"How many times he gotta hit on me 'fore he run out of chances?" I asked her.

She took a deep breath. "You know you can't go back to the apartment, right? I told you before, Robert ain't gonna allow this mess. Ain't nothing more I can do." She sat down on the bench.

I looked down at her now. Looked like she was worn out just from talking to me.

"If you ain't here to help me, why you here?" I asked her.

"Robert told me this morning some money was missing out of his pocket. I told him it must have fell out. But then I saw you were gone. Knew you'd be heading back to Milwaukee or trying to find your daddy. When the police showed up at my job, I nearly had a heart attack."

"You come looking for me when you saw I was missing?" I asked but already knew the answer.

"Robert said to me, 'If he want to go so bad, then let him go.' So, I did."

"My ma was right—you ain't no kind of momma," I screamed.

She raised her hand to slap me, but then sat back in her seat staring with water in her eyes.

"Why'd you bring me to Chicago if you didn't want me here?" I asked her.

"Ain't no one said I didn't want you. You been sitting up under your grandma and grandaddy so long, you think I'm supposed to be your maid and not your momma. Time you learned how the real world works and learn some respect, Lymon." She pulled a handkerchief from her purse to wipe her eyes.

"This here's the real world?" I yelled again. "Look where I am, Momma!" It felt like my whole body was on fire. A police officer looked in at us through the window. Thought he was gonna come and take me out, but he walked away, probably used to yelling. "Your husband beating on me all day long, and you pretending not to see?"

She sat quiet shaking her head saying, "You don't understand."

"You always done that?" I asked her then.

"Done what?" she asked, looking down at her hands.

"Walk out every time something gets hard? Like you did when I was a baby?"

"Lymon, like it or not, I'm always gonna be your momma," she said. "Not your grandma and not your aunt Vera, just me."

The officer came in. "Let's go," he said, and took me into the courtroom.

THREE

Chicago, Illinois 1946

"LOOKS like you've gotten yourself into some trouble at home," the judge said from up high behind a big wood desk in the front of the courtroom. Standing there alone with one police officer beside me, and another up near the judge, felt worse than being in the principal's office. But I knew this was going to be a lot worse than getting in trouble for fighting. The judge coughed as he looked down at a stack of papers in front of him and the light shined off his bald head. With his little round eyeglasses, he looked as old as Grandpops.

"No sir," I said.

His voice got louder. "There was some money stolen from the home of Robert Hassell? And you were found at Union Station, attempting to board a train, is this correct?"

"No sir, that money was from my aunt Vera and—"

"In addition to running away, you were suspended from school on October seventeenth of this year?" he asked, sounding tired.

"Well, yeah, but…"

"Says here you have a history of truancy." He looked right at me, his little eyes looking over the tops of his glasses.

Truancy was the word the man used when he came by the house to talk to Ma 'bout me missing so much school.

"No sir, I go to school every day," I told him, feeling the sweat running down my back.

"Not according to these records," he said, lifting up the stack of papers.

I heard a door open in back, and I turned to look. Momma walked in. She sat in the back row.

"My momma is here," I told the judge.

"Miss Caldwell," the judge said to her, waving her forward.

She stood up and walked to the front.

"It's Miss Pitts, but Mrs. Hassell is my married name," she said, almost whispering. When she got close, I saw her face was wet with tears.

"Where's the boy's father?"

Momma shrugged her shoulders. "He's here and there, Judge."

"Momma…" I said soft, hoping she'd tell the judge 'bout Robert and Daddy and Ma getting sick and me moving to Chicago, but she stared straight ahead at the judge, sniffing and wiping her eyes.

The judge cut in. "It appears that there is very little parental control in the boy's home. The court believes, that given the gravity of the charges, it is in the best interest of this minor to be remanded to the Arthur J. Audy Home for a period of four months. At that time, the court will make…" The judge kept talking, and I couldn't make myself understand what he was saying. Only way I could tell it was bad was watching Momma's head shaking from side to side. Could see her mouth saying, "No. No.…"

I tried again. "Momma…" *Where was I going?*

The officer took my arm.

My momma finally looked up at me. "I'm sorry, Lymon," she said.

I realized now, wasn't no going back, with Momma or anywhere else I knew. Wasn't no more "hangin' on," waiting for Daddy or God or Aunt Vera.

"Tell my daddy," I yelled at her. "Can you at least do that? Tell my daddy where I'm at!"

I broke then. Seemed like tears I didn't know I had came pouring out of me like a busted pipe.

"C'mon, son." The officer pulled me forward. I used my free hand to wipe my face and my nose as I watched my momma walk out the courtroom.

———•———

Police officers put me back in a car. They were talking and laughing up front like wasn't nothing wrong with me riding to a home for boys. A prison, just like my daddy. Never saying goodbye to Errol, Theo, and Orvis. I laid my head against the cold of the window. Didn't know how I was gonna start all over again.

I closed my eyes tight as I could, hoping to hold back the tears I knew would start again if I thought about it long enough. But I think I just 'bout cried myself out back in the courtroom.

We pulled up in front of another big brick building, 'bout the biggest I've seen in Chicago.

They walked me up the steps, through the tall front doors, and down a long hallway, past a roomful of boys. Most my age, but some older, just a few younger, all turned to stare as I walked past. I made sure to stare right back.

FOUR

Arthur J. Audy Home
Chicago, Illinois 1946

JUST like at school in Milwaukee, I kept to myself. After he gave me a talking to about "rules" and "behavior" and "expectations," Mr. Pinker, the head of the Audy home, had one of the younger boys show me where I'd sleep.

"Name's Marshall," he told me when we left the office.

"Lymon," I said. He looked about Orvis's age and I couldn't help but wonder what he could have done to end up here. I followed along behind him to the Colored Boys sleeping room lined with cots, one next to the other. Looking down that long row of beds made me think of visiting day with Daddy back at Parchman.

"You gonna sleep on the end here." He pointed.

I nodded. Each cot had one pillow, and one thin blanket. He showed me my locker that had a towel and washcloth, soap, and a toothbrush.

"They'll give you your clothes later. Don't expect much. They give us stuff don't nobody want, but it's clean." He shrugged. Was like Calvary Baptist clothes all over again.

"And you know we got to go to school every day 'cept Sunday, right?" he said. "Classes are on the other side of the building."

I sat down on the edge of my cot.

"Can't sit here now. Time for lunch. Free time is later." I stood up and followed him to the cafeteria. Wished now I hadn't complained 'bout Momma's cooking 'cause the food here made me wish I could have one of her dry pork chops now. I sat by myself, watching the other boys and making myself eat watery stew and a piece of dry bread. Seemed like all the older boys stayed in one group, and they were the loudest. After a while, I got so tired I could barely keep my eyes open.

We scraped our plates and stacked our trays, then free time started, and I went back to my cot and laid down. Was so loud in there, I didn't get much sleep, but I was glad to finally be alone again without someone yelling or fussin' or lecturing on what I should or shouldn't be doing. Looking up at the ceiling, stained brown from water and who knows what, I tried to think 'bout what was next for me, outside of the Audy Home. Couldn't go back to my momma's. Milwaukee seemed so far away, didn't see how I could ever get there. I couldn't let myself hope my daddy would come, 'cause it was the hoping that made the hurting worse. I remembered all those years I went without him while he was at Parchman. But with Grandpops with me every day and night, I didn't feel so alone. Wondered if I'd ever feel that way again. The blanket was scratchy and hard, and I turned on my side and tried thinking of something else, anything to stop thinking 'bout all the sad, and that's when I heard the music.

Sounded like it was coming from the cafeteria and I sat up. One of the bigger boys was walking by.

"What's that?" I asked him. "That music?"

"Band practice," he told me, and kept walking.

I made my way back to the cafeteria. The tables and chairs were moved against the wall now, but it still smelled like the nasty food we just ate. There were boys every age with instruments I never seen before. Everything shiny—horns, round plates. In back was a boy with a drum hanging from a belt 'round his neck. The man at the front was young with wild, curly hair looked like it hadn't been combed in a month. Didn't help he kept running his hands through it. He looked at me over his little eyeglasses when I came in.

"You here to join us?" he asked.

"Nah, just listening," I told him. I had my eye on the boy with the drum, but he pointed to the other side.

"We need some help here in the brass section," he said. Those instruments looked big and heavy. I shook my head no.

"Everybody wants the drum," he said, smiling. "But we've only got one of those. Have you ever played a trumpet?" Everyone was looking at me.

"No," I said quiet.

He waved to a boy in back. "Clarence, hand me yours." Clarence was tall and skinnier than me and was about the whitest-looking colored boy I ever seen. He walked up and handed it to him. Looked like one of the horns from the night-club. The teacher took a cloth from his back pocket and wiped the end you blow into. He played the start of the song Grand-pops loved called "Ain't Misbehavin'," and I laughed. "Louis Armstrong," I said loud.

Back home, Grandpops played his records every now and then. Ma didn't much like him. Said she hated his ole scratchy voice, but Grandpops said he could play his you know what out of a horn.

"You got it. That's Satchmo's instrument. You know your music. Here, give it a try." He wiped it off again.

This time I blew, but didn't sound nothing like him or Satchmo. Everybody in the band laughed now, but not the mean laughing I heard in school.

"Everybody sounds like that the first time. Takes some getting used to, but you'll get it. Right, Clarence?" Clarence nodded, then came up and took back his instrument.

"Why don't you sit there and observe for today, and then we'll talk about getting you your own."

Seemed like everywhere I go, music was following me. I sat down and listened, wondering what it'd feel like to have my own instrument again and be part of a band.

FIVE

Arthur J. Audy Home
Chicago, Illinois 1946

FOUND out Mr. Danforth was the name of the band teacher. He was young, someone said, just finished college. Guess he couldn't get any other job teaching if he had to work at the Audy Home. But he loved music 'bout as much as I did. Maybe more. He'd get so worked up at practice, he'd sweat right through his shirt.

I was hoping there'd be a guitar somewhere, but Mr. Danforth said we had to work with what the state gave us, and that was band instruments.

"They want to make sure you boys understand discipline, not appreciate music." Seemed like we were doing both, but Mr. Danforth seemed mad when he said it. When finally he handed me a trumpet, all shiny and pretty, it felt like Christmas morning and my birthday all rolled into one. Made me almost forget about my broken guitar. Almost.

I been struggling to read words my whole life, but I never thought I'd have a hard time reading music. Thought music was something you played not read.

"If you are ever going to be a serious musician, Lymon, you are going to have to know how to read notes," he told me. He pulled out sheets of paper from his satchel and sat them on a stand.

"How am I gonna read this?" I asked him. It looked like a page of lines and circles. Mr. Danforth was real patient. Not like the teachers in school who told me I wasn't smart. He laughed and pointed out how each note on the sheet matched up with the note on my trumpet. "Open position, one and two, one and three, open position…"

"Playing guitar ain't this hard," I told him. "My grandpops taught me and we didn't look at any papers. "

"Sure, that's one way to play," he said. "This is another. I understand you won't be with us for very long, so let's make your time here count for something."

'Fore I knew it, reading music was easier than reading a book. "I knew you'd get the hang of it," Mr. Danforth said. He said I caught on faster than most. Mr. Danforth said what Grandpops did, that I had "an ear."

At the home, every breath I took was on the clock. From the time I opened my eyes till I laid down on my cot at night, the dorm father, the teachers, even Mr. Pinker, all kept watch, making sure we got up at one time, went to class at another, and ate that nasty food three times a day. We got to shower only two times a week. For some that meant washing up at the sinks in between, but for a lot of the boys, they just waited, and that meant we all had to smell their stink for the other five days.

But every Tuesday and Sunday was when we had practice. Woodwinds, the drum, and my section, brass. Can't say I cared for the songs, each one with that steady drum beat in the back. It was music for marching, not dancing. I laughed thinking about Mister Joe trying to sing to this music.

Once I got the hang of my trumpet though, I started practicing even when there was no practice.

When I had a hard time and hit wrong notes, Mr. Danforth reminded me, "I know it's not the same as playing the songs your grandfather taught, but now, you can continue to learn new songs because you know all of the notes." I thought my grandpops would like that, and I kept right on trying.

Me and Clarence didn't talk much outside of Mr. Danforth's class, but together, side by side on our trumpets, it was like we had our own language. I may have been stuck up in this place, but playing music with a roomful of boys in a band made me feel 'bout as free as a bird.

SIX

Arthur J. Andy Home
Chicago, Illinois 1946

I was practicing on my cot, when Clarence came to get me.

"You got a visitor," he said.

I kept right on playing. "I ain't got no visitor."

"Mr. Pinker sent me to get you." I saw he wasn't joking, and I got up and headed to the visitor's room. Hardly anybody gets visitors here, and I saw just 'bout everybody watching and whispering as I walked down the row of cots. I walked down the long hallway, to the office where Mr. Pinker was waiting. He took me into the visitor's room. He pointed to the clock. "Thirty minutes, son."

I saw him from behind, hunched over in a jacket that looked too big.

"Daddy?" He turned and looked at me. Not smiling. He stood and for the first time we stood eye-to-eye. I wrapped my arms around him. Took him a minute, but then he pulled me close. I rested my head on his shoulder.

"I'm here," is all he said. "I'm here."

He led me over to the corner and we found two chairs.

"How you making it, son?" Daddy asked.

"I'm making it," I told him. Daddy tried to smile, but it wasn't nothing like his big one.

"Your momma got word to your aunt Vera. Wish I could have been here sooner."

"I'm sorry, Daddy," I said. "I was trying to get back to—"

"You don't owe me nothing," he said serious. "You waited, just like I told you to. Problem is, I made you wait, when it was my music should have done the waiting."

Daddy talked to me 'bout everything he could think of. Everything except why I was there. And I was glad 'cause that was the last thing I wanted to tell him. When he started in 'bout the places he'd been playing, I stopped him.

"I got something to show you," I told him. "I'll be right back." I ran down the hall, nearly slipping on the polished floor. Everyone looked up when I went back into the dorm with the cots. Some faces were looking sad, like they were wishing they had a visitor too, but I couldn't think 'bout that now. I picked up my trumpet and the sheet music and ran back to the visitor's room. Time I got back to Daddy I was out of breath.

"What you got there?" he asked, looking at what I was holding.

"A trumpet!" I told him. "Mr. Danforth, he put me in the band here. I ain't that good yet, but I'm getting the hang of it."

"Well, let's hear what you got," Daddy said, sitting up straight, like he was sitting at the Regal Theater.

"Here?" I asked, looking 'round. The room was mostly empty, but now I wasn't sure I wanted my daddy hearing me play when I was still hitting so many bad notes.

"I gotta wait till you at Carnegie Hall?" he asked, laughing.

I put the trumpet to my lips, set the sheet music on a chair, and played the "Stars and Stripes" song I'd been practicing for weeks. I didn't look at Daddy, just the music when I played, so I could play my best. When the song finished and I looked at my daddy, he sat quiet.

"Told you I wasn't that good yet," I said, putting the trumpet down on the chair.

He shook his head. "I'm just thinking, I hope you blew loud enough so your grandpops could hear you up above, 'cause I know you making him proud."

"Not in here I ain't," I said, sitting down.

"Lymon, he forgave me. He'd forgive you too. You made a mistake, same as me, only difference is, you got a lot more time to make it right. Looks to me like you're doing just that."

"That mean you liked my playing?" I asked.

"You got a gift, son. We just gotta make sure you use it right. Maybe one day, when you finish up your schooling, the two of us will have to go out on the road together." He drew out our names in the air. "Grady Caldwell and Son."

"How about Lymon Caldwell and Dad?" I asked.

Daddy grabbed me by my neck. "Why you gotta take top billing? You trying to say you better than your old dad?"

Daddy sat me down. "Listen, before I go, I got some news for you. Clark got me a job down at the foundry, so I'd have something steady. I moved Ma back into the house. Only thing missing is you."

"You mean I'm going back with you and Ma?" I asked him. Not wanting to let myself believe it like before.

"Sure are. But the folks here said you got two more months you got to stay and then they can release you to my custody." Daddy whistled. "You hear that? They gonna release *my son* to *me*? So, looks like now, I'm waiting on you." He smiled, sad around the edges.

"Why can't I go with you now?" I could hear my voice choking.

"Law's the law, son. Know I told you that before. You broke it, now they aim to break you."

Daddy put his hand on my knee. "You come this far, Lymon. Just a little more to go."

"You talk to my momma?"

He shook his head no. "No more than I had to. I'm bound to end up in here 'longside you if I see that husband of hers."

"They don't let old people in here." We both laughed.

His voice got lower. "You're gonna see your momma again one of these days, and when you do, I'm trusting you'll both see things a little bit clearer."

"Not so sure 'bout that," I said.

"Sometimes even grown folks got growing up to do." Daddy cleared his throat. "I know something about that."

He looked me at me straight.

"Now I'ma tell you up front. It ain't gonna be easy with Ma. You think she was fussin' before? Woowee...that woman give the devil a run for his money!"

I laughed again.

"Gonna need the two of us to keep things in order. She's missing you something bad. She needs more than me and Vera to fuss at all doggone day. Vera said she'll help out best she can. It's what Pops would have wanted. Us working as a family is what would've made him proud, right?"

I nodded my head.

Daddy looked up at the clock. "I gotta get a move on if I'm gonna make that train. You keep practicing and I'll be back before you know it."

SEVEN

Arthur J. Audy Home
Chicago, Illinois 1946

NEVER got a chance to say goodbye to my daddy when they took him to Parchman, or my grandpops 'fore he closed his eyes one night and never woke up. Seemed like when it came to people who mattered, there was always something that came between me and moving on. But on my last day at the Audy home, I finally had my chance to say what I needed 'fore I was leaving for good. I hadn't made friends here like Errol and Clem, but there was something about being in this place, knowing we were all in the same mess, made me feel closer to the boys in the band than I ever felt to anybody. Together we found music, or maybe music found us. Maybe they had a daddy or a momma telling them to hang on, that things were gonna get better. Maybe not. But for all of us, it was music that gave us some hope when everyone else let us down. And Mr. Danforth. He took time with me like I was someone worth taking time for. So, after I stripped all the sheets off my cot and said my goodbyes to everyone in my dorm, spending extra time with Clarence, I walked over to Mr. Danforth's office with my trumpet.

"You all set?" he asked.

"Yessir," I told him.

"Well, I know you're not sad to be leaving this place, but I'm sad to see you leave, Lymon. You've been a huge asset to our band and—"

I couldn't wait for his words when I needed to tell him mine. "Thank you, Mr. Danforth. For everything you taught me. Not just about music either. But when you were helping me, it reminded me of learning the guitar for the first time with my grandpops."

"Well, you inherited a lot of talent from your grandfather I suspect."

"And my daddy," I reminded him.

"Of course, and your father. Wish I could let you take that trumpet with you, but…" He held out his hand to take it.

When I handed it to him, I hugged him at the same time and the trumpet hit his back. He looked a little surprised by the hugging. I was too.

"Well, thanks again, Mr. Danforth."

I walked out the office and down the hall and waited on the bench outside Mr. Pinker's office. I thought, seemed I spent more time waiting for my daddy than being with my daddy.

While I was waiting, another new boy came out the office with Marshall, who was showing him to the dormitory.

"What time's your daddy coming?" Marshall asked me.

"Be here any minute," I told him, looking at the big clock in the hallway.

"Okay then," he said, nodding goodbye.

I didn't know time could go by so slow. Just 'bout when I started wondering if this was gonna to be one of those times when I'd have to wait for the wind to change, the front doors to the home opened, and my daddy walked in, smiling big.

———•———

I barely let him take two steps 'fore I was on him, hugging hard as I could.

"If you choke me to death, you ain't never gonna get out of this place." He laughed. "Wait here and let me go sign these papers," he said, and walked into the office.

I waited some more, but this time it didn't feel like no time at all. When he came out, I asked, "We taking the train back?"

"Nah. I got a ride from a friend." Daddy picked up my bag. Wasn't much to it, just a few sets of hand-me-down clothes the home gave me.

We walked down the hall together and stepped outside. The weather had finally started to get warm again, felt like summer was just 'round the corner.

Out at the curb, a car was waiting. The door opened on the driver's side, and a tall man with white hair stepped out.

"Mr. Eugene?"

He came forward and shook my hand. "Looks like this head hasn't been touched since I seen you last." He smiled.

"Don't think it has." I smiled back.

"Well, let's get you back to Milwaukee, and we'll see what I can do," he said to me, taking my bag.

I climbed into the backseat with my daddy up front.

Mr. Eugene turned on the radio and turned the button past all the talking and the static till he got to music. He stopped when he heard a guitar playing.

"That's that new Muddy Waters song," my daddy said.

Mr. Eugene stopped playing with the radio buttons then, turned up the sound and pulled away from the curb. We all sat back listening.

> *Well, it gettin'*
> *Late on into the evenin'*
> *and I feel like, like blowin' my home…*

We drove past houses and some of the streets I knew. Past all the stores and clubs, past St. Lawrence and out of Bronzeville and Chicago and to the highway. Mr. Eugene drove smooth and easy, and slow enough so I could try and read the signs. Finally I saw one that said WELCOME TO WISCONSIN.

I didn't even look back.

Us

ONE

Milwaukee, Wisconsin 1946

When we pulled up in front of the house, Daddy had to shake me awake. "We're here, son," he said, rubbing my head. The house looked smaller and broke down, but I couldn't wait to get inside.

Mr. Eugene got out and took my bag from the trunk. "See you Saturday?" He winked at me.

"Yessir," I told him.

"I've been doing all the cleaning since you left. Let's just say, I'm gonna stick to barbering." To Daddy he said, "Third Sunday's next week, Grady. The men's choir will be needing your help."

"Yes Lord, don't I know it." Daddy laughed. "I heard you all last month."

Mr. Eugene shook our hands hard and got back in the car. After he pulled off, we walked up the front steps, and Daddy opened the door. I held my breath. The house was quiet.

"Where is she?" I whispered.

"In back," he said. "Ma, we're here," Daddy said out loud.

I set down my bag and walked to our bedroom.

Ma was sitting up in bed and I ran to her. She looked the same as I left her, but next to the bed was a chair on wheels.

"Careful now," she said when I leaned in to hug her. I looked down where the blanket was flat next to her one leg.

"Does it hurt?" I asked her, still whispering.

"I don't feel a thing," she said. "Well...stand up and let me look at you."

I stood and she was quiet. Her eyes took in every piece of me.

I turned to look for Daddy, but I could hear him in the kitchen.

"Ma—" I could see the water in her eyes. "Ma, you okay?"

"I am now," she said. I sat back on the bed next to her. "You know they got me in this chair now to get around," she said. "The doctors said they wasn't sure I was gonna make it. Shows you how much they know." She smiled, tired. "I wasn't sure you'd want to leave Chicago to come on back to Milwaukee. Your momma..." Ma stopped and took a breath. "Sounds like you had a time there."

I nodded. "Chicago was nice, but I'd rather be here with you and Daddy."

"Now let me tell you something." Ma sat up straighter in her bed, fixing her nightgown. "I told Grady, I don't need to hear all the goings on about what happened with your momma, her husband, and that home. Your grandaddy would have said,

'What's done is done,' but I'm not gonna stand for any foolishness here in my home."

"Ma, I know. I'm not gonna—"

"Don't tell me anything you can't do. You act up here, you can take that mess right on back to your momma and Chicago." Ma's voice started getting louder.

"I don't want to go back." I looked her in her eyes. She looked so small now, sitting in bed. Her eyes were watery with dark circles underneath. Sitting here on her bed, she looked a lot less scary.

"I learned to play the trumpet," I told her.

"Mmm-hmmm…" she said. "I don't mind you playing, but you got to remember I need my rest too. You and Grady know this ain't no juke joint. Can't be playing all hours of the night."

I put my head down then. "Ma…I don't have Grandpops' guitar. It's gone."

Ma closed her eyes. Looked like she was praying.

Heard her say, "…no kind of sense."

"It wasn't my fault," I told her. "Maybe it was. I was trying…"

Ma put her hand on mine. "Your momma ain't got no kind of sense. I told Grady from day one, that woman ain't never gonna be any kind of mother. But he didn't want to lis—"

I remembered Daddy telling me one day me and my momma gonna see things different. I don't know if that day is ever gonna come, but one thing for sure, it ain't coming for Ma. Before she got going good, I asked her, "You want anything from the kitchen?"

She stopped her talking about my momma. "Help me get into this chair. Ain't no telling what Grady's doing in there. He'll have this whole house burned down."

Ma wasn't light as I would have liked, but she wasn't heavy either. She showed me how to turn her so I could hold her under her arms and lift her into the chair.

Ma ain't never have anything good to say about me, so when she said, "You getting strong," I had to smile.

I tried to push her chair, but she smacked my hand away and pushed herself turning the wheels. She was faster in the chair than she was on her feet.

In the kitchen I saw Daddy had moved around everything so Ma could get to it. Kitchen table was all the way in the corner, and most of the food was in the bottom cabinets so she could reach. Ma told me and Daddy to get on out and she started cooking supper.

TWO

Milwaukee, Wisconsin 1946

TWO years in Chicago, and Milwaukee looked the same as when I left it. Daddy took me over to see Aunt Vera and Uncle Clark, and 'side from Aunt Vera looking bigger around the middle and her hair getting white 'round the edges, even she hadn't changed. She just 'bout kissed me to death. Only this time, she had to stand on her toes to reach my face.

"Look how big he's grown, Clark," Aunt Vera said, like Uncle Clark couldn't see with his own eyes. "And handsome too." I hugged her tight when she said that. She didn't say nothing 'bout my momma or the Audy home. She even made me my favorite coconut cake and put some candles on top too.

"It ain't even my birthday." I laughed.

"I know, baby, but I missed a couple," she said, kissing me some more.

I ate just 'bout half the cake myself. When Daddy told me to slow down, Aunt Vera hushed him. "Let the boy eat," she said.

Just like Daddy promised, he's been going to work every day at the foundry with Uncle Clark. He don't look happy going, but when he comes home, if he's not too tired, or just finished working a double, he'll take out his harmonica and show me how to play. Daddy says he's working on getting me a new guitar, but I miss the trumpet too. Hoping I can get that on my own with the money I'm earning at Mr. Eugene's. First day back in the barbershop, after all the customers left, Mr. Eugene asked, "You remember where I keep the rags?"

"Yessir," I told him, going to the closet in back. But Mr. Eugene stopped me.

"I been thinking about our arrangement," he said. I got scared thinking he changed his mind about me working for him.

"I told you I had to do my own cleaning while you were gone." I nodded, holding my breath. "Well, son, I think it's time we discussed a raise." Hearing him say "raise" made me think 'bout my momma and Robert, but I kept nodding.

"Starting today, I'm gonna pay you a little something every week *plus* one haircut. How does that sound?" I kept nodding. "Thank you, Mr. Eugene."

Mr. Eugene laughed. "Don't thank me yet. Dirty as this place is, chances are you'll be asking for another raise before you're through."

Mr. Eugene was telling stories. The shop was about the same as when I left, probably cleaner. But I did just like I used to, wiping down everything in sight.

I climbed into the barber chair soon as I put everything away, and Mr. Eugene came and stood behind me. 'Stead of reaching for his scissors, he put both his hands on my shoulders and looked at me in the mirror.

"Mind if we talk a minute?" he asked me.

Whenever grown folks are asking questions, I know it's gonna be something I don't want to answer.

I nodded my head to the mirror.

"I know you had a time back in Chicago," he started. I breathed in loud and heavy, hoping this talk wasn't gonna take long.

"Before you start that huffing and puffing, I got something I want to tell you." Mr. Eugene turned my chair to the side and sat in the chair next to mine.

"A few years back, when I was your age"—I smiled even though I didn't want to—"I got into a little bit of trouble," he said.

"You?" Mr. Eugene didn't look like the type who was even late for school.

"Yeah me. I was young and hardheaded. Started hanging out with some knuckleheads."

"What happened?" I asked him.

"Well, that's what I want to talk to you about. It doesn't matter what happened then. All that matters is what happens now," he said.

I nodded.

"Do you understand what I'm telling you, son?"

I nodded again. "You saying, don't worry 'bout the past?"

Mr. Eugene said to me, "You know what happens when you spend too much time looking behind you and not enough time watching where you're going?"

"You fall down and break your neck," I said.

"I knew from the moment we met, you were smart." Mr. Eugene smiled.

He stood up and turned my chair back to the mirror. "Now let me see what I can do with this mess," he said, taking out his scissors.

THREE

Milwaukee, Wisconsin 1947

I kept going to church with Aunt Vera. Not to get out of the house with Ma like my daddy said. And not for the coffee cake like Mr. Eugene said. And not because I needed God in my life like Aunt Vera said. I went because of the music.

My daddy's been going to help out the men's choir, but this week, when I got up to get dressed, Daddy said he was tired and staying home.

"You best bring some cotton for your ears," he told me, lying on the couch. "I can sing loud enough to drown out most of them, but you in trouble this week."

My daddy was right. They weren't the best singers, but their voices were loud and deep, and the congregation clapped and threw their hands up in the air just the same. Mr. Eugene was the tallest, and when they started swaying from side to side, some of them bumped into each other 'cause they couldn't keep time. The choir director mouthed all the words and moved her hands telling them when to speed up or sing softer but didn't look like none of them were even paying attention. But even while I stood clapping with everyone else and listened to Aunt Vera singing along loud in my ear, I was looking at Miss Minnie on piano. She rocked from side to side on the piano bench. I could see she had sheet music, turning the pages with one hand while she kept playing with the other, but I don't think she even needed to follow the music. Made me think 'bout Mr. Danforth at the home and how he told me I could learn the notes for any song if I knew how to read music. When Miss Minnie played, sometimes she was looking at the choir, sometimes at the choir director, and sometimes she even closed her eyes and tilted her head all the way back. Her playing made even the men's choir sound better.

"...the grace of God and love of the Holy Spirit be with you all."

When service ended and Reverend Lawson said his last words of the Benediction, I made my way out of the pew.

"Gimme a minute, Aunt Vera," I said and hurried up through the crowd up to the front. Miss Minnie was still sitting at the piano bench talking to one of the deacons. I stood and waited till they were done.

"You Vera's boy, right?" Miss Minnie asked me, closing the cover over the keys.

"Yes ma'am. I'm her nephew, Lymon."

"Vera need something?" she asked, gathering up her music.

"No...no ma'am..." Back in the pew, I had in my head what

I wanted to say, now I wasn't so sure. "Any chance you could teach me how to play piano?"

Miss Minnie stopped moving and looked at me. "I'm no piano teacher, Mr. Lymon." She laughed. "I know how to play, but that don't mean I know how to teach."

"I'm a fast learner. I played my grandpops' guitar and a little bit of trumpet, but I always wanted to play the piano."

"Vera know you asking about piano lessons?" she asked.

"No ma'am," I told her.

"Then I expect you want to learn pretty bad, you asking without permission."

"I expect so," I said.

She was quiet.

"Let me think on it a little, Mr. Lymon, and I'll have an answer for you next Sunday. How's that sound?"

"Thank you, ma'am," I told her.

"I didn't say yes. I said I'll think about it. And I'm gonna be speaking to Vera."

When Aunt Vera dropped me back at the house, I ran inside to tell Daddy about Miss Minnie and the piano. Ma was up and in the kitchen cooking dinner, and the whole house smelled like navy beans and ham hocks and cabbage. I ran in the kitchen.

"You know better than running in this house," Ma said.

"Sorry Ma. Where's Daddy?" I asked.

"He left out when he got up. I ain't seen him."

I went on back to the small bedroom to change out of my

church clothes. The day I came back from Chicago, Daddy told me to put my things in the small back porch off the kitchen. We mostly kept some broke-down things there and the room was cold in winter with wind whipping through the cracks. But me and Daddy worked to clean out the room and put all the junk in the backyard. I swept it out good and Daddy bought a small cot and dresser and some extra blankets. He even let me keep our old radio on the dresser.

"Don't play it loud and don't play it late," Daddy told me. "This ain't no juke joint," Daddy said in a voice like Ma's.

"It ain't much," he told me, "but a young man can't be sleeping with his grandma."

"But Ma's gonna be scared," I told him.

"She'll be all right. I'm out here on the couch, and you back there on the cot. We can hear her just fine," he said.

I was sure Ma would fuss 'bout being alone, but she didn't say one word. Seemed to like having the room to herself. I know I did. Wasn't much to look at, but it was the first time I had a space all to myself, without having to share a room or sleep on a couch or with a roomful of boys since Grandpops died.

I folded up my clothes neat and went into the front room. Daddy didn't tell me he was going anywhere. My stomach all of a sudden was tight and bubbly. I sat down. Next to the flowered couch where Daddy slept was a bag where he kept some of his clothes. The little closet near the door was where he kept the rest. I made sure Ma wasn't watching as I got on my knees and opened up Daddy's bag just a little to see inside. Far as I could tell most of his clothes were there. Then I walked to the closet, looking over my shoulder at the kitchen door for Ma. Since she's been in the wheelchair, she moves so fast, I sometimes don't hear her. I opened the closet door slow so she couldn't hear the squeaking. Saw Daddy's workclothes hanging next to his one suit. When I was closing it back, Daddy walked in the front door.

"What you looking for?" he asked me, wiping his feet on the rug.

"Nothing...I was looking...for my jacket." I turned away.

"What would your jacket be doing in my closet?" he asked me, not smiling.

I didn't answer.

"You hear me talking to you?" Daddy said mad.

I shook my head, but I couldn't look him in his eyes. "I thought you were gone," I whispered.

FOUR

Milwaukee, Wisconsin 1947

MA wheeled to the door when she heard Daddy yelling.

"Grady, what are you fussing at this boy about?" she asked.

"This don't concern you, Ma," he told her, still staring straight at me.

"You in my house, and you telling me it don't concern me?" she said loud.

"This is my boy!" Daddy yelled. "And I got a right to talk to him as I see fit. Leave us be, Ma."

I was waiting for Ma to get up out the chair and pop Daddy in his head. But she backed up her chair into the kitchen.

"What do you mean, you thought I was gone?" he asked me.

I thought 'bout all those times Daddy came for the day and left before I got up, never saying goodbye. Or when he just passed through on his way to another gig, rubbing my head and making me laugh, but never ever being a daddy I could count on. Just like my momma, I spent most of my time waiting on someone to make things better.

Even when I got tired of waiting, soon as he showed up, seemed like he made it right again, till he didn't.

When I stood in front of my daddy now, my head was just a little bit higher than his. "I don't know if you're staying or not," I told him.

Daddy looked like someone let all the air out of a balloon.

"We family, Lymon. I told you, things gonna be different now."

"How many times you told me that and left in the morning?" Even though Daddy was talking soft again, I could hear myself getting louder. "How many times did you leave without even saying goodbye?"

I could feel the wet on my cheeks, but I didn't even know I'd started crying. "I came home to tell you about the piano and Miss Minnie, and Ma said you'd gone and I…" My hands curled up tight in a ball.

"I ain't gonna leave you again, son," Daddy said soft.

"How many times you said that?"

Ma was in the kitchen quiet, listening.

"How could you leave me in Chicago with my momma when you knew…I should've been with you and Ma. And you left me there with Robert beating on me. I didn't have no daddy to fight for me." I ran out of words.

Daddy looked down at my balled-up hands.

"You wanna swing on me?" he asked.

I shook my head no, but I wasn't sure I didn't.

"Grandpops would have never—" I started again.

"I ain't Pops," Daddy said. "Never tried to be. We both lucky to have had him, but there's only one Pops."

I opened my hands.

I was breathing hard and Daddy took a step closer. "You know I'm gonna take care of you now. You and Ma. You know that, right?"

He was wanting me to say yes, and wanting me to stop being mad, but I'd been hanging on to promises so long, I realized back in the home there was only one person I could count on. And it wasn't my daddy.

"I know that when I ain't got no one else, I got me. I know that." I told Daddy, looking in his watery eyes.

He nodded his head up and down. "Well, you right about that," he said so soft I could barely hear him.

Ma started moving again in the kitchen, banging around pots like we didn't know she was just listening.

"I know you're mad, son. Got every right to be. I'm asking you to give me another chance, is all," Daddy said.

Daddy hugged me tight and I let my arms stay by my side, not ready to hug him back. But Daddy didn't let go. He smelled like smoke and sweat, and I breathed in deep and laid my head on his.

When he let go, I walked through the kitchen to my room and sat on the cot. I turned up the radio loud enough so I could just hear it. I laid back and stretched out my legs long. With my eyes closed I listened to the guitar on the radio and could see Grandpops holding me on his knee while I played guitar.

You got it, son, that's it. I heard his voice in my ear.

On my legs, my fingers played along to the music on the radio.

Author's Note

When I created the character Lymon in my debut, *Finding Langston*, I never imagined he would have a starring role in his own novel.

Initially, I believed Langston's nemesis, the seemingly angry, small-minded bully Lymon, was beyond redemption. But as I encountered readers of *Finding Langston* who wanted to know more about Langston's tormentor, I began to ask myself the question: *Are bullies born or are they made?* As the story of Lymon emerged, the closer I came to an answer.

Both Langston and Lymon began their lives in the rural South, in communities fortified by family and faith. Both had loving, nurturing relationships with their grandparents. And they both fed their inner lives through a love of poetry and music. It was their move North that provided transformative experiences. Through circumstance or chance, their worlds collided at a time when neither was able to see their common bonds.

After reading Jesmyn Ward's powerful novel, *Sing, Unburied, Sing,* the idea of intertwining the stories of Lymon, his father Grady, and the Parchman State Penitentiary (also known as Parchman Farm), was born.

Parchman Farm opened in 1900, and by 1937 housed nearly two thousand inmates. Some were as young as ten years old. Prisoners were underfed, subjected to corporal punishment, and allowed family visitation only on fifth Sundays, which amounted to four days per year.

Most families boarded the Midnight Special train, which traveled through small Delta towns to Sunflower County, Mississippi. Prison superstition held that the first convict to see the lights of the approaching Midnight Special would be the next set free.

Parchman was home to several famous names, including blues greats Son House and Bukka White, who wrote and recorded "Parchman Farm Blues" after his departure.

I was haunted by my further research into the history of the notorious prison, which uncovered stories of countless black men serving extended sentences for minor offenses and being forced to work in the scorching sun for fifteen-hour days in the convict-leasing system. Lessees, such as railroad companies or wealthy landowners, paid fees to the state for the convict labor to farm acres of cotton, clear land that was often in malaria-infested swamps, dynamite tunnels, and lay railroads. Incarcerated inmates were at a dramatically increased risk of infection, disease, and death. This system was a financial windfall to the state of Mississippi and became one of the state's greatest sources of revenue with yearly multi-million-dollar profits, which in turn led to increased arrests and convictions to keep up with the demand for labor.

Once prisoners were released, they faced Jim Crow laws. The sundown towns that Grady references were white communities that enforced strict segregation and fear tactics to exclude non-whites. A black person's presence in the town after the sun set could lead to arrest or worse. Between 1890 and 1940 nearly two hundred of these towns existed throughout the country.

The parallels between the history of the convict-leasing system and our current prison systems are at once startling and unsurprising. While much has changed in the eight decades since the fictional Grady would have served his time at Parchman, much has stayed the same. Namely, the disproportionate numbers of African American arrests, the higher conviction rates often for less serious infractions, and the longer jail sentences, again for less serious crimes.

Today, the subsequent impact of incarceration on the families that prisoners leave behind is also apparent.

Though *Finding Langston* and *Leaving Lymon* are historical fiction, both are rooted in the troubling histories of the Jim Crow South and reveal how this system adversely affected their lives as well as the lives of future generations of millions of African Americans.

Langston and Lymon arrived in the Northern Midwest from the South during the Great Migration, a period in history where large numbers of blacks flocked to cities in the North. Both young men had loving, yet complex relationships with their fathers that played out in dramatically different ways. I liked to imagine that perhaps in another time and place, they would have been friends.

The forces that shape us and the world around us can be random and, at times, cruel, but the legacy that matters more than any other is a legacy of love, community, family, hope, and finding the music of life, wherever you land.

Lesa Cline-Ransome

Acknowledgments

Thank you again to the entire team at Holiday House Publishers, but especially my editor, Mary Cash, for helping me to find the story within the story.

And to all of those who patiently answered questions and provided much-needed information—Elvera Ransom, Kim and Leif Roschell, and Eduardo Vann.

My amazing reader, Joan Kindig, who combs through every sentence and punctuation mark with love and care.

For friends and family, who read and comment and support—Lisa Reticker, Ann Burg, and Leila Ransome.

For Cheryl Logan, who over breakfast at a café in Lenox, Massachusetts, jotted down a plan that helped me to find time where I thought there was none, and transformed my writing life.

And to my agent, Rosemary Stimola of Stimola Literary, thank you for your trust, patience, and advice. For Rhinebeck's Starr Library and their patience with my overdue books. For authors David Oshinsky and Timothy Tyson, whose powerfully honest works shine a light on history and injustice.

And always, thanks to my family who cheer me on every step of the way—James, Jaime, Maya, Malcolm, and Leila Ransome; and Ernestine, Linda, and Bill Cline. Our memories lead me to the heart of each story.